As I replace the letter in its envelope, anxiety mingles with pleasure. She must not find a tired, lonely old man. At least in letters one can dissemble a little, rationalise one's life, pretend to an equanimity one does not possess....

Everything was so different when she last visited. I it was who had chosen rightly; soon to be citizen of a proud young nation. She had married into an Empire that was everywhere in retreat. What glory the future held in store, for Singapore and for me. For her there could surely only be regrets, the loss of home and family, the warmth of St John's. She had given up so much for Charles ... to my chagrin, of course, but by the time of her visit I had long since overcome my jealousy.

Abraham's Promise

Abraham's
Promise

Philip
Jeyaretnam

University of Hawai'i Press
Honolulu

Front cover photo by Albert Lim KS
Back cover photo by Tuck Loong

Published in North America in 1995 by University of Hawai'i Press
2840 Kolowalu Street
Honolulu, Hawai'i 96822-1888

First published in Singapore in 1995 by Times
Books International
an imprint of Times Editions Pte Ltd
Times Centre
1 New Industrial Road
Singapore 1953

© 1995 Times Editions Pte Ltd

Printed in Singapore

95 96 97 98 99 00 5 4 3 2 1

Library of Congress Cataloging-in-Publication
Data

Jeyaretnam, Philip.
    Abraham's promise / Philip Jeyaretnam.
        p.   cm.
    ISBN 0-8248-1769-9 (alk. paper)
    I.   Title.
 PR9570.S53J483   1996
 823--dc20   95-30290
                                       CIP

Acknowledgements

To the Fulbright Foundation who delivered me from legal practice for four glorious months in 1990/91 and gave me time to start this book; to Shawkat Toorawa who patiently read this book when it was twice as long but only half as good; to Shirley Hew, for having faith in me; to Falaq Kagda, master of the semicolon; and most of all to Cindy, who keeps my heart dancing and my legs aching struggling to keep up with her ...

For Father

It is folly alone that stays the Fugue of Youth and beats off
louring Old Age.

Erasmus
The Praise of Folly

One

To endure three score and ten years once seemed the greatest possible victory. History is written by its survivors, survival elevated into triumph. Yet now that I near that full measure of my days I have discovered the flaw fatal to this happy scheme of things: longevity alone is not enough. He who captures the minds of the young is in truth the victor. And the young are so impressionable. A generation of new students, perhaps their passage into teachers, another generation of their students, and all that I have lived by will be forgotten. Even my Victor, my son Victor, is a stranger. Quite uninspired by my dreams, my old-fashioned ideas: knowledge for its own sake, virtue its own reward. Young, hard and ambitious, with the capacity for success that I have always lacked. Yet what will he succeed in? The amassing of wealth? The accumulation of power? Nothing of any true worth. His success will be my final failure.

I am old and grey, and it is all I can do to muster my thoughts from far-flung melancholy, from childish rage at my own son's assurance, and press them into duty in pursuit of the interest and attention of the young lad who sits before me. Not to mention of his parents' wallets. "There can be no fine thoughts, no nice agonies of conscience, until a man has bread in his belly." Krishna, you old rogue, you always had an answer. Every departure from principle and right conduct could find its necessity in your silver tongue. But you at least I have outlasted.

Perched at the dining table, hands clasped in front of me, I wonder how I look to the boy. He probably sees me as all bones, and indeed my skin is taut across the protruding knuckles. With my head bowed, and my scalp showing beneath my thinning hair, I probably look like a monk to him. I am convinced that I frighten him. Old men always frighten young boys, perhaps for good reason: we are what they must become. And so they fear us, or else despise us; two sides of the same coin. I must wax less philosophical, concentrate on the moment, show him that I am not to be feared. Respected yes, but feared no, or else I risk losing him, this my first pupil in over a year. Is he hard inside, like Victor? They cannot all be like that, not from the beginning. It is education that turns them so. Perhaps I can still reach out to him. After all he's chosen to study Latin. A boy who wants to study Latin cannot be beyond redemption.

"In two years' time or so you will sit the 'O' Level. That may sound a long time away, but if you want to do well, as I'm sure you do, you must work hard now. Your parents tell me this is the first time you are studying Latin?"

"That's right."

At least the boy has answered, and in a clear and steady voice. I make eye contact now, looking up at him, over the black frame of my spectacles. Was it always so difficult? Did teaching always feel like this, as if one were a charlatan about to be unmasked: the old pontificating to the young when their own lives have fallen so short? I must halt this querulous speculation. It is not helping.

"That is good. You will have no bad habits to unlearn. But you must want to learn. Latin is like anything else. You struggle at first, you may feel frustration when you can't learn everything at once,

12

but in the end, when you have mastered it, that's your reward. You want to learn?"

"Yes, Mr Isaac."

"Latin is a wonderful language. Like English, it is the language of conquerors. And like English, it has been the vehicle for the spread of the Gospel."

The ceiling fan revolves slowly overhead, stirring the air just a little, without any great enthusiasm. This is my fault: I asked for the speed to be reduced, for nothing would make my task harder than having my papers fly hither and thither as I seek to address the boy in a calm, dignified and yet inspiring manner. In front of me a glass of cold water gathers drops of condensation. They swell until gravity sets them trickling down the side of the glass. Thankfully the mother-of-pearl coaster on which it stands has a rim which stops the pool of water from leaking out across the polished rosewood. If not, the Primer that I have opened between us would face a threat from a different element. And as usual my attempts at foresight would be rendered nugatory.

"The Romans won for themselves a great empire. They started out as a band of wanderers, who escaped from the ruins of Troy after that city had been sacked by the Greeks. The story is told in *The Aeneid*, an epic poem by Virgil, which we will study. Part of it in any event. In the end this band of wanderers settled on the seven hills of Rome, a city no bigger than Singapore."

The boy is staring at my lips. Either he's impressed, or he's noticed that I forgot, in my rush not to be late for this first lesson, to put in my dentures. Struck by how solemn he looks, and anxious over what his thoughts may be, I almost forget what I am about to say. Somehow, all my years of teaching perhaps, I recover my composure.

"Gradually they subjugated the whole of Italy. Then they fought a number of wars with Carthage, where Hannibal came from. Carthage was in North Africa, and victory over Carthage brought the Romans control over the whole of the Mediterranean Sea. Then they expanded north. The army, commanded by Julius Cæsar, conquered Gaul, the name for France in those days. We will read part of his account of these conquests. Even the island of Britain fell to the Romans. Now, boy, why do you think that the Romans were so blessed in their conquests?"

For a moment I think that he's not going to answer, that his thoughts are wholly adrift, and I hesitate between patient repetition and harsh rebuke. Before I come to a decision, he speaks.

"I don't know. Why?"

"For the spread of Christianity. The Roman Empire served God's purpose by establishing a common language for the preaching of God's word. What language was that?"

"Latin, sir." Good, he is following. Yet I'm still worried about the impression my words may be having. This link between language and religion always worked in the mission school in which I taught, but I am aware how unsophisticated it is to insist on such a connection, especially today, when the young seem so protected, so spoilt, yet somehow so worldly, so confident. Soft in their self-indulgence, yet hard in their lack of illusions and ideals. How can they accept the possibility that God's mysterious ways might be so transparent, so reducible to the logic of evangelism? I am not at all sure that I do.

"Yes, good. Not Hebrew. Not Greek. Latin. Christianity spread to Britain in the language of the Romans. And then, more than a thousand years later, the British Empire brought Christianity to the world. In English. You understand?"

He's nodding. He understands.

"So that is why it is good that you should learn Latin. Open the book now. Yes, chapter one. We will start with the first conjugation of verbs. Do you see that table? You must learn how verbs change their endings depending on their person, tense and mood. Person and tense I'm sure you understand. Mood I will explain another day. It's all very simple really. You have a root, in this case 'am', 'a', 'm', and then you change the endings to make your meaning. 'Am-o', I love; 'am-as', you singular love; 'am-at', he, she or it loves; 'am-amus', we love; 'am-atis', you plural love; 'am-ant', they love. You must learn in this way. Understand?"

No doubt he does. He's probably convinced that Latin is boring and mechanical, and that I'm a withered old man who will teach him by force of repetition, whether he wants to learn or not. He must regret his decision to embark on the subject. Or was it his parents'? Did they insist? I know how you feel, I want to say, I was young once too, but stop myself just in time. Part of a teacher's advantage is to seem different, to wear the authority of difference. I am here to make you like I am. A man schooled in the ways of the world. Experienced and assured. A stern but loving father whose guidance, where necessary, extends to the rod. But is that the kind of teacher I wanted to be?

My own father, standing over me, yes, with a rod, over Mercy and me, for we were both, in a concerted effort, refusing to eat the rice and curry that Mother had prepared. Father's voice always slowed at such times. Explaining in measured tones how many hours he had to work to put each meal upon the table. How many hours of shuffling paper, dealing patiently with hospital administrators, Englishmen who knew nothing about how the place was kept running, who only knew that they, by dint of their skin colour, commanded the people like my father who were the cogs and wheels of the system. How old was I then? At an age when fear of Father was beginning to change into a desire to emulate him, when love of Mother was transforming into contempt for her weakness, holding Father's arm and crying that he should not beat us. Certainly it was I who took the first mouthful of food. Mercy, her eyes fixed upon me, received the beating.

I am glad when the lesson ends. It's so long since I have taught, tutored, whatever, that at first I hardly knew what to say. Lack of practice, that's all, made me feel an imposter. After a while the old rhythms began to return, the adjustment of pace, form and content in sensitive response to the pupils' mood. Teaching for me was a calling, a desire to guide the young and unformed into knowledge and understanding. Without the rod. The modern world, I believed, must abjure the old ways. The arrogance of those who ruled, keeping their subjects safe and reasonably prosperous, must give way to the democratic participation of all. Colonialism was fading, its shadow diminishing, and young saplings of independence were thrusting into the sunlight. Youth, days of power and possibility. Yet in the end was it not I who was out of step with the world? I, believer in the necessity of freedom, who was fundamentally out of joint with society? Must security and comfort always be preferred to the rigour, the pain, of thinking for oneself? Must we always fear our inner selves too much to allow our outer selves true autonomy? No wonder I could not remain a teacher.

Two

The day after the *Prince of Wales* and the *Repulse* arrived at the Naval Base is a day I will never forget. At school everyone was talking about it; that and the Australian troops who had also just arrived.

Gopal, the son of a lawyer and the natural leader of the class, was pretending to be an Australian soldier whose bush hat had been knocked down over his eyes so that he could not see. He was blundering around, banging into desks.

"Strewth, not fair, you Nips ... leave my damn hat alone ..." He grappled with an imaginary enemy.

The door swung open. Gopal scrambled back to his place in an instant. Absolute silence, everyone at attention at their desks. Mr Motilal glared angrily around the room, his black-framed spectacles sitting awkwardly, slightly askew, on his bulbous nose, giving him a cross-eyed appearance. His shoulders were rounded and slumped forward, making a hump of his shoulder blades. He was North Indian, and so never would have understood, even had he known of it, the Tamil nickname *ottagam,* meaning camel, given to him by Gopal, and gleefully adopted by the rest of the class, even the Chinese, Malay and Eurasian boys. Everyone knew that the cause of Mr Motilal's anger was the same as that of our merriment. He was vexed because the arrival of the British ships and the Australian troops clearly indicated that the British would not let Singapore, their prize possession, slip from their grasp, and that, to save us, they would defend the whole of Malaya. How could the Japanese now dare to strike across the Gulf of Siam from their new bases in Indochina?

It was an open secret that Mr Motilal sided with the Japanese, and looked forward to a Japanese-led war of Asian liberation from the White Man's domination. Even the school principal, a soft-spoken, red-faced Welshman, Mr Thomas, apparently knew of Mr Motilal's leanings and viewed them with an amused tolerance.

"Sit down, boys."

Mr Motilal taught geography. He stood now by the blackboard, his large nose in profile, staring at the globe that faced him from the other side of the blackboard. He turned towards us.

"Today we will revise Lancashire, the industrial heartland of the British Empire. What are Lancashire's chief industries?"

Gopal answered first. "Theft, sir, theft."

"Don't be funny, boy."

"No, sir; theft of cotton, jobs and money from India."

Mr Motilal smiled for the first time that day. "Very good, Gopal, but not an answer for the examinations. Textiles is certainly one of Lancashire's major industries. What are the others?"

Those days of preparation for war were etched in vivid reds, whites and blues. There were red, white and blue flags along Coleman Street, flying from lampposts, as the Australian troops passed through, heading upcountry in their large two-and-a-half-ton trucks, covered in green canvas. And in harbour, indomitable and proud, were the mighty capital ships of the Royal Navy.

But that bold blue moment of euphoria, speckled with red and white flags, did not last much beyond the arrival of the *Prince of Wales* and the *Repulse*. Early one morning, about four o'clock, sirens awoke me, drawing me to the window, where I stood transfixed by the sight of Japanese aircraft, in the neatest of arrow formations, flying high in the sky, illuminated by searchlights yet apparently invulnerable to the puffs of anti-aircraft fire. Bombs were dropped in the centre of the city, and hundreds of civilians killed or wounded. Not one Japanese aircraft was downed. Even now I remember how my anger mingled with excitement, and even admiration, for those daring aviators.

Memory, having swept me back to the heady days of the War's eve, now drops me indecorously back in the present. I am seated at my desk, facing the row of books that stand against the wall between dusty bookends — large ungainly wooden elephants whose tusks have long since broken off. The spines of the books are marked by frequent use. The pages are yellow, blotchy and discoloured. Looking at these repositories of learning, my best friends, I pity their sufferings from our heat and humidity. Scholarship can never conquer in these parts: every seeming victory is mocked by the steady workings of the climate, a climate that rots wood, paper and fabrics with democratic indiscrimination. Perhaps it was always a hopeless battle — and with that thought comes anger, momentarily shaking my body, reminding me of my increasing frailty, leaving me slumped in the chair.

I have at least a new pupil, although he is less a prospect for scholarship than a source of much-needed lucre. Anything would be better than having to depend on Victor. My son has done so well, has sold his soul so readily to the marketplace, has turned his back so firmly on all that I stand for, that I must never give him the satisfaction of contrasting my parsimony as a father with his generosity as a son.

So the income from this tuition I will set up like a bund around a padi field, to control the dissipation of my shrinking pool of savings. Two afternoons a week means a hundred and fifty dollars, enough to cover most expenses, including the rent on this room.

Perhaps we might manage thrice a week. But to secure that, I must first ensure the boy's interest. His eyes (when they were not wandering off towards the sliding glass door that opened onto the back garden) seemed to be blank most of the time. Is he just a fool, a rich boy without an interesting thought in his head, or can he be a dreamer, his thoughts in flight all afternoon? Why on earth is the boy studying Latin? No one values knowledge for its own sake any more. But then what can the reason be? His father's command, perhaps, based on the belief that the rigours of Latin can knock discipline into the most feckless of souls? If the boy is a fool, the more likely alternative, hard work is his only hope, and the only cure. But if Richard is a dreamer, although hard work remains essential, I must also find some way to spark the boy's imagination, to set the fires of his mind burning towards his Latin texts.

When I first studied Latin, it was very much by rote. Declining and conjugating with such ardent repetition. As with mathematics, it took a long time before the patterns began to form of their own accord. Only when Mr Clarke took over the class did I really begin to understand the magic of the language, a language of conquerors and poets, of centurions and eunuchs. Mr Clarke was a great bear of a man: red face, heavy cheeks, big belly ... I think he was drunk most of the time. I don't honestly know how he kept his job. Sometimes you could smell the whisky on his breath even in class. But inside that bear of a man was an exquisitely fine mind of enormous sensitivity. He used to read Virgil aloud, rolling the words off his tongue, keeping the metre with a wagging finger, and his face, his ruddy, thick-jowled face, would be transformed, exalted. … Sometimes it was all I could do not to laugh, but at other times I trembled upon the very edge of tears. The funny thing was that he seemed to teach better when he was drunk. When he was sober he was terribly impatient. But when he was drunk, even the slowest could keep up, because, whether he was aware of it or not, he kept repeating himself.

It was Mr Clarke who first made me understand that only in something that is wholly useless, utterly irrelevant, can we glimpse true beauty, the beauty of the divine.

Three

$\mathcal{M}$y wife's photograph, framed in silver, catches my eye. It's funny, it's been on my desk for so long that it usually doesn't register in my vision. Once my sleeve has wiped the dust off the glass, her eyes sparkle, and I bring the photograph closer to my eyes to examine her lips pouting to cover her front teeth, her dear, darling teeth that in moments of doubt she would berate in the mirror: "You refugees from a rabbit warren, go and curse someone else's face." She could never believe that I delighted in her mouth, in the hesitancy, the vulnerability, that the thrust of her teeth imparted to her lips. She would cover her mouth with a hand when I said such things, or tuck her chin into her shoulder, shielding her lips from my gaze. Gradually though, little by little, enduring the tempestuous tossing of her head, I would work my lips towards hers, until finally our lips were joined. "Rani, my dearest." The words slip out, as if they are just part of an ordinary exhalation of my breath, yet still somehow they find an echo, a hollow echo, in this bare room. It has been so long, so long since I felt her touch, smelt her scent of sea air, sandalwood and musk; so long that I spend weeks, trapped in the grind of my everyday routine, the daily chores that swallow up the hours, weeks without a thought of her, as if she belonged to an age long past, a dream from which I have long ago awoken.

The photograph is in black and white. But I remember her sari: the deepest of reds, with a pattern of flowing leaves marked out in gold thread along its edge. The picture was taken at Albert's Studio in Stamford Road, soon after we were married, before Victor was born. By then I had been teaching for some years, teaching English and Latin at St George's. We drove there in our white Morris Oxford. The school holiday. Chatter, light-hearted chatter, as the car sped towards the studio, my window down all the way in spite of her protests that the wind would ruin her hair, hair which she had spent an hour oiling and combing. For a moment, the rush of air is once again on my cheeks, and yet, perhaps I have confused another occasion, another drive. Does it matter?

We had a number of pictures taken, some together, some apart. One of us together I particularly remember. She seated, I with my arm on the back of the chair. Her chin raised, gaze a little distant, lips formed in that characteristic pout. I stared directly into the camera, a severe, stern expression on my face. A young man, strong, sure of myself. It was the age of independence, the age for men of independent minds. But where is that picture? Victor had one copy made for himself, but the original should still be here with me somewhere.

The trunk at the foot of my bed hoards papers and brown envelopes, infusing them with the smell of mothballs. The disorder makes me uneasy, for it affords myriads of hiding places for memories. They lurk within, ready to seize me should I reach inside. I distrust the grip that memory, sparked by some chance reminder, can exert, throwing me into melancholy, longing or despair. Yet I must see that photograph.

I lift out an envelope, which looks promising, the right size for photographs. But it contains only letters. The handwriting ... of course, they're from Rose, Rose Chinappa, who wrote so diligently after she left for England with her Englishman.

My dear Abraham,

The sea stretches endlessly in all directions. How insignificant I feel, adrift on this vast ocean. It is as if this great liner were no more than a cork bobbing on the surface of a pond. What more proof is needed of the grandeur of the Lord's work?

Yet, even though the sea seems without end, suddenly we arrive at our port of call, and we are returned to a human scale and perspective. I have been told that tomorrow we land at Colombo, and I shall be posting this letter from there.

Charles has taken such good care of me. Of course I never expected otherwise, yet somehow each new kindness takes me by surprise, and sends a little wave of happiness rolling through my heart. We both have First-Class cabins, and are treated by the stewards as I used to imagine only royalty might be. I do so wish you had come to see us off: you would have seen my cabin then and I would not have to describe it to you.

The bed runs half the length of one wall, and has a wooden railing to stop me from falling out at night. Perhaps if the seas were rougher it might prove its usefulness, but thus far it has served only as an obstacle to my getting into bed each night! The sheets are starched white cotton, changed every day, and there is a top sheet below the blanket, but folded over it at the head of the bed. I didn't dare tell Charles I'd never seen a bed made up like that before! There is a porthole on the other side of the cabin from the bed, through which I can see, even as I write, blue sea and blue sky, barely distinguishable one from the other. I am sitting now at a little table, not really a proper desk, and I have my books arranged in front of me, including, may I say, your kind gift of the Bible.

It is all such a contrast from the voyage I was on when last I left Singapore. Do you remember our earlier parting? On that boat all was fear and uncertainty, loved ones left behind to face those dreadful Japanese, who only days before had sunk the Prince of Wales and the Repulse.

Today, by contrast, I am sailing into a new future. I hope you will come and visit us in our new home, one day. But first, find yourself a good Christian girl to look after you. And work hard at Teachers' College. May God bless your endeavours.

Yours ever,

Rose

In spite of my reluctance to reawaken childhood desires and youthful lusts, I reach at once for the next letter, beguiled by an image of Rose, smiling, her long, black hair pinned up into a bun.

My dear Abraham,

It was wonderful to see Sushila again. How close we became during those four years, those dark years of the Occupation. Now

25

she is married, and has a baby girl! Imagine! Of course, I knew, as you know from her letters, that she had delivered, but to see the adorable creature in her arms, that's a joy. And she's Joy too; that's what they've named her. She has such bright eyes and chubby cheeks, and the most mischievous smile I've ever seen, unless one counts that cherub in the Annunciation in St John's, the one to the right, who looks more like he's going to drop the lilies onto Mary's head than hold them aloft in her praise.

I also met George, her husband. He is dark, with thick eyebrows and bushy sideburns, rather quiet really, but I dare say he is a good person. His father is a priest and has such a loud voice and firm handshake, the complete opposite of George, who seems quite shy. George's sister, Shantini, has married Sushi's brother, Joshua, and he has now found a good job in Service. I did not meet them, however, since we were in port for only one day, but at least Sushi has now met Charles, after all my letters about him, and I have met George, and George's father, and little Joy.

Charles is working hard every day. He says that the last three years he has been out of touch with events in England, and he says that, as in Malaya, there have been many changes. But at least there is no more rationing in England. Charles tells me not to expect too much, that England is not as grand as I think, it is not all palaces and gardens, but I cannot help being excited. And so is he. He will not admit it, but I know, I can tell he is excited because he has not seen his family for three years and now he is bringing home a bride. What will they think, Abraham, of their Tamil daughter-in-law? I am a little scared of this, of meeting them. Do you think I am brave, Abraham, as I like to think, or am I just foolish? Will I be back with my tail between my legs, as Father says?

But I must not trouble you with my fears. I believe Charles when he tells me everything will be all right.

Please write to me when you can. I do not want to lose your friendship.

May the Lord bless you, Abraham.

Yours ever,

Rose

My eyes hurt a little — the writing is just a little unfamiliar in its youthful neatness. Rose's handwriting has grown bolder, bigger, wilder, with the passing years. The old pain rises in my heart, the pain of parting, of losing her. Charles, slight, frail, pale Charles, yet with a strength of voice and manner that captivated her. He was with the Colonial Legal Service, coming out soon after the War ended. Lived off the River Valley Road, riding a trishaw to the Courts each morning, his immaculately turned out grey suit and white topi an impressive contrast with the trishaw, whose metal frame was polished by its pedaller with black shoeshine till it gleamed and sparkled in the early morning sun.

Charles attended St John's, where Rose and I sang in the choir, seated across the aisle from one another. I am sure she really did look especially beautiful that first morning when Charles joined the congregation, the sun streaming through the windows behind her, highlighting the sheen of her hair, her eyes dancing and her bosom heaving as she sang.

Charles spoke to Rose afterwards, at breakfast in the church hall. They were out of hearing, but I saw her smile, her mouth opening to laugh. Annoyance, anger, quickly overwhelmed by helplessness. Did she know, ever really know, how I hungered for her, how she haunted my dreams, that fine long neck and cascade of hair, her small, even, white teeth? How could she not know, when I stared at her across the aisle each week, she smiling each time I caught her eye, tossing her head back a little as if to give her voice more room? But I was just a little boy, all of two years her junior, first singing in her row, then, after that one year's absence from the choir as my voice broke, across the aisle. How could she look upon me with anything other than amused affection, or sisterly concern?

Four

The evening after that first air raid the Chinappas came by, the parents bringing with them Rose and her elder sister Lily. The parents went inside, leaving Rose and Lily out on the verandah with me. Mercy, as ever, had to help serve the guests. This she did in her usual reluctant, hesitant manner, as if she had been called upon to perform a difficult and dangerous feat. She should have been a boy, for her awkwardness made her a clumsy hostess. Even when there were no guests, and she helped Mother in the kitchen, her efforts always seemed on the verge of disaster: she would allow water to boil over or drop the plate her hands were blindly drying. But that evening at least, as far as I can recall, there was no mishap. Did she serve tea that day? No, I'm sure it was ginger beer, and crackers perhaps, Jacob's cream crackers. When she had finished, Mercy came out onto the verandah to join us.

It was the last half hour of daylight, when a boy's thoughts turn to dinner. The Chinappas' arrival meant that dinner would be delayed, and I was anxious to know what it was that had brought them uninvited to our house at such an inconvenient hour. And with all four of them in such solemn procession. But Lily's presence kept me silent. I was always intimidated by her. The four years by which she was my senior, and perhaps even her younger sister's friendship with me, made me in her eyes an entirely undesirable companion in conversation.

Rose spoke first. "We have booked tickets for the passage to Colombo. We will be staying with relatives there until the Japanese have been sent packing."

The back of my throat went dry. To speak seemed impossible.

"Appa and Amma think your family should come too. At least you and Mercy and your mother."

In the late afternoon sun the shadow of the house reached a long way down the gravel driveway. Into that shadow came a sudden chill. Then a moment of silence, broken by Mother's voice, calling for Mercy. She stood up and went back into the house.

At last I found words, but dared not look at Rose. "You know my father won't want to leave ... the hospital may need him."

"Appa also said he couldn't leave, at first, but Amma talked him out of his stubbornness."

"But my father doesn't work for himself like your father, he's at the hospital. I heard him telling my mother yesterday that he can't ... won't leave as long as the English doctors stay. After all, they're the ones the Japanese would ... you know ... if they ever ..."

Rose lifted up her head. She was sitting on the verandah step, on the edge of the garden, while I was now standing a little to her side. She wrinkled her nose, and my knees weakened. In that same moment I was stirred to anger, for she had no idea of her effect on me, and suddenly it seemed intolerable that she should, without even knowing it, hold such power over me.

"I hate the Japs. Funny little men. Why are they so greedy, why don't they stay at home?" She spoke in a pouting tone of voice that I had not heard from her before.

If Father stayed, Mother would too. Would Mercy and I then be sent on our own to Colombo? Near Rose, safe from bombs and all those dreadful things that the Japanese had done in

China and now appeared to plan for the rest of Asia, yet cut off from all the action. But why bother to weigh the advantages and disadvantages of going or staying? The fact was that my fate lay in the hands of my parents. Whether I went with or was separated from Rose was no doubt being decided at this very moment, and decided with no suspicion that the question of leaving for Colombo could not, in my mind, be framed in any other way. Again the knowledge that my passion was locked away, cloistered from the world, from Rose even, enraged me. Looking away from Rose I answered her question with another, hardening my voice into carelessness.

"And the British? Why didn't they stay at home?"

Now at last Lily, who had been sitting at a distance, unconcerned and aloof, spoke.

"Abraham, you really are a silly little boy. Everyone knows the British came here with the Bible, doing the Lord's work. The Japanese are heathens. You know what they did to the Christians in their own land — they crucified them, hundreds and hundreds by the roadside. And you know what they've been doing in China. Listen, boy, they'll do the same thing here if they ever get the chance. If you want to stay here and be their friend, please don't let us stop you, but please don't involve Rose or myself."

I was about to join battle, roused, notwithstanding my usual trepidation, by the insult, when Rose caught my eye. So I kept quiet, putting my hands in my pockets and staring at my feet. Mercy reappeared at that moment and sat down beside Rose. "What's the matter? Why is everyone so quiet?"

Rose put her hand on Mercy's arm. "I think we're all a little strained. We'll be leaving soon and perhaps we shouldn't talk, should just listen to the birds." Rose paused, and sure enough the birds had begun to chatter, gathering in the trees in the garden as darkness fell. "I hope you will both come to Colombo."

Lily shot a single, narrow look at Rose. I caught it from the corner of my eye, as I stared into the darkening sky in which stars were beginning to appear. It was a look of warning, warning Rose not to patronise her. Still, Lily kept her silence, and her distance. After a few moments I sat down next to Rose, on the other side from Mercy. A light evening breeze was ruffling the trees, whose dark crowns were silhouetted against the sky. Once the darkness settled in, the birds quietened, conceding the night air to the cicadas. Mercy stood up to fetch a mosquito coil, which she lit and placed to one side of the verandah. Its fragrance drifted among us, as we sat there between the insects humming in the darkness-enshrouded garden and the adults whispering in the lighted interior of the house.

That feverish sleepless night it seemed that the lives of millions hung in the balance, and, among them, mine and Mercy's. I could not sleep, nor, I imagine, could Mercy, after our parents told us that we would be sent to Colombo in the care of the Chinappas. To Colombo, where we could stay with our mother's sister, whose husband was in Service.

I tossed and turned all night, too hot with the blanket covering me, too cold with it off. Rose was in my mind that night, as in so many nights since. Most of all her scent as she sat beside me on the verandah, the smell of talcum powder freshly applied after a bath, but also something else altogether, something much more exciting. Was that the night I first imagined unwinding her sari and laying my head between her cool breasts? Such thoughts could only have made it harder for me to sleep, and when I did so, perhaps only when dawn was poised to break, it must have been to dreams of her, perhaps to the dream of her that recurred so often during the dark days of the Occupation, a dream of a boat, rocking gently on the seas, the two of us rocking gently together, rocking with the waves, until suddenly the boat was sinking, the sea sucking us down into its murky depths ... and I would fall back into consciousness with a jolt.

We did not go to school the next day. The rickshaw man who normally took us to school was paid his wages for the week and given a note to pass to our school principals.

That day became a day of packing. Mercy and I had a sturdy metal-framed trunk each. I started with my clothes, and my shoes: my spare white canvas shoes and my black leather shoes for church. Mother gave each of us a photograph, taken the year before. She was seated, Mercy resting awkwardly in her lap, while Father stood behind and slightly to the right of the high-backed chair, one hand resting on its back. I stood in front of Father, the grasp of his other hand secure upon my shoulder. Where is it now?

No matter how hard I worked at packing my trunk I felt I could never complete the job, let alone set sail for Colombo. Every so often I would wander over to the window. The glass was dirty, as if the impending hostilities had made Mother neglect her domestic duties, as if the threat of war made all such activities dwindle into insignificance. The window was streaked with dirt and its sill lined with the remains of tiny insects and fragments of leaves. I stared out at the garden, at the rambutan tree, which would soon be heavy with fruit, whether the Japanese reached Singapore or not. What a shame to miss this year's rambutans, or did they have them too in Colombo? What trees, come to think of it, did they have in Colombo?

It took Mother's intervention to get my trunk packed. Where I dithered, daunted by the number of things, unsure what to pack or in what order, she, after the obligatory scolding of my sloth, packed fast and neatly. When she had finished, she called me over, and, ruffling my hair, showed me where everything was: underclothes, sarongs, shirts, shoes, Bible. Over them all she laid out a blanket, folded in half. "It may be cold on the ship."

Was it that day or the next that Father came home in the late afternoon and gathered the family about him in the front room? I approached reluctantly, expecting a family prayer in anticipation of our parting. I did not relish the prospect of tears from Mother, who might even be joined in them by Mercy. Not that I displayed my reluctance, for Father's command was law.

We formed a solemn circle around Father, seated in his armchair.

"The *Prince of Wales* and the *Repulse* are sunk. The Japanese have landed near Kota Bharu."

He spoke abruptly, in a firm voice, without preamble. Mother wailed, "How? How can it be?" until Father spoke to her, quickly and sharply, shifting into Tamil to make the point more strongly, telling her to pull herself together and not scare the children. Silenced, Mother sat down on one end of the settee. For some reason I was more excited than scared, even as my mind burned with the thought of those great grey vessels, fiery coffins, sinking fast beneath the waves, flames that singed the lungs of the crew doused only by the drowning sea.

"As a result of that the whole town is panicking. I went to the shipping line offices but there are no tickets, for love or money no tickets."

Father's words stand out against a backdrop of Mother's tears.

"I went to see Chinappa. He's made me an offer which I have accepted."

Mother looked up, a sob dying on her lips.

34

"He will give me his ticket. So there is one berth. For Mercy … or for Abraham." The pace of his words accelerated. "Abraham is the elder. It will be easier for him to live without us in Colombo. Are you ready to go?"

I looked from Father's anxious, uncertain face to that of Mercy. Her lips were pressed tightly together, a thin, pale line, as if set in stone.

"What does Thangkaichee want?" I stammered over the words. When Mercy said nothing, I looked back at Father, Mother, and then once more at Mercy.

"Mercy?" It was Father, his voice quiet.

Finally she spoke, her eyes fixed on him. "I will stay with you."

Mother, wringing her white handkerchief, now broke her silence. "But Mercy is a girl. She will be safer in Colombo … we do not know with these Japanese …"

Father stood up. He walked to the window and tapped his fingers on the sill. Looking out into the garden he spoke again.

"Amma is right. Mercy will go."

I too stood up. The air felt so close and damp, and Mercy's sullen silence so oppressive, that I had to go outside, where at least there might be a breeze. Why she was not happy to be delivered from the hands of the Enemy I did not try too long to understand, for my thoughts were already turning to my imminent separation from Rose.

Five

Like so many other nights of my past, tonight is troubled and sleepless. That night on the eve of war, when I believed myself bound for Colombo. Another night, driving through the rain, in search of Mercy. And then that night when I stayed in bed instead of following Rani into the empty midnight streets. This night, of course, is more commonplace, just another night when I wander back over my life and its many turnings. Surely my life can withstand any scrutiny: it has always been an examined life, at every step I directed my energies towards becoming a good son, good brother, good husband, good teacher and good citizen. There cannot be many others who, awake in their beds at night, may honestly share this boast. But then why am I not rewarded with the grace of sleep, calm repose after a lifetime's toil?

Today was not a good day. First of all, the Yeos' car was not on time to pick me up from the bus stop at the edge of the estate where they live. Fearful of missing a lesson, and the remuneration that comes with it, I began to walk in, struggling with the incline of the hill. I had almost reached the point at which hopelessness sets in, the increasing number of rests required seeming proof of Zeno's theorem, when the Yeos' Mercedes pulled up, its smooth purr mocking the rasp of my breath.

The boy was in the back seat, smiling in welcome, or perhaps laughing at my frailty, my painfully slow gait. The Malay driver reached over and opened the front door, gesturing for me to get in.

It took me an age to do so, and when I had finally settled into the seat and tried to pull the door shut it did not close properly. The driver then spoke to me in a most insolent manner. *"Tak tutup."*

I opened the door and tried to slam it. The double click told me it had not fully closed, had rebounded from the catch.

The driver sighed. He undid his seatbelt and reached across me, pushing my hand away from the door handle. He opened the door and slammed it hard. As he buckled his seat belt once again and put the car into gear I heard him say, softly but distinctly, no doubt intending to be overheard, *"Orang tua."*

I attempted to fix the man with a glare invested with the authority of my vocation. But the driver kept his gaze on the road ahead. If I am old and grey-headed, at least I am an old teacher. Surely age establishes the depth of my learning. I deserve respect, even if I have to force my tired old body to walk in the hot afternoon sun in order to earn my daily bread. What is the world coming to?

After that beginning how could the lesson go well? The boy's boredom was on display in his long, lingering sideways glances towards the sliding glass door that leads to the garden. It was, perhaps, only to be expected: with Latin one has to build a solid foundation first, only later does it become enjoyable, the game of detective when reading a dense Latin text, striving to catch nuances and resolve ambiguities.

But how to explain all of that? That room, the carved wooden frieze nailed to the wall, stolen originally from who-knows-what temple, the marble floor, and, under my feet, the hand-woven silk carpet. How can I explain to that boy, who no doubt has only to express a wish for it to be granted by his indulgent parents? How to tell him that one has to work hard now in order to secure future gains? For Richard, studying Latin is probably a whim which will soon fade away. In my day I kept my nose to the books, even in the midst of the Japanese Occupation, when, my schooling interrupted, I had to work as a translator. In spite of this, I still studied, at night, devouring any books I could get my hands on. Yes, even when I was tired from a long day at the Transport Ministry, always at the beck and call of that young Japanese officer (what was his name now — Kamaguchi or Hamaguchi?), constantly being called upon to explain peremptory orders to bewildered civilians. I studied, dreaming of liberation, of the day when the rule of law would return, and I could start life again. I worked, suffering in the present for the sake of my future.

How can I explain that to this boy, this child weaned on television, on programmes that consist of a succession of flashing numbers to teach one counting, pictures to teach words and the alphabet, and cuddly animals acting out short scenarios that express simple moral lessons? For this boy education has to be entertaining, has to be fun. But real education is not like that: education, like medicine, is something good for you, no matter how bitter its taste. A teacher can do little to sweeten the pill, only seek to inspire his pupil to make that extra effort of ingestion.

Mankind, in the name of progress, lightens his burdens with each passing generation. Automobiles to travel in, calculators to do our counting, microwave ovens to do our cooking. At the touch of a button the accumulated toil of millennia whirs into service of the humblest individual. It is supremely democratic, yet its levelling has reduced us all. Comfort turns us sedentary, weakens our characters and softens our backbones. While the race grows ever more powerful, capable of destroying the entire world at the touch of, yes, another button, the individual becomes more feeble, more narrowly conscribed in his competence. Who can be hunter, farmer, cook and homemaker? Let alone doctor, engineer, lawyer and teacher?

On a handful of specialists (themselves incompetent outside their speciality) our abilities in any field rest. On the complex workings of a system no one person can rightly comprehend, let alone control, our comfortable lives depend. Even our storytelling we now leave to so-called professionals, to the vast production of drivel that spews forth daily from our televisions. Drivel because to entertain all, it cannot upset or challenge anyone.

So if I am an old man, unable to open a car door, incompetent in the modern world of buttons and machines, I am still no worse than any other, no worse than that insolent driver, slave to the gears and levers of his machine. And in my mastery of Latin I have chosen precisely that speciality on which nothing depends, thus freeing myself from the chains of the system. I am not driven, like so many others, into justifying my life in terms of the extent to which others need that fragment of mankind's inheritance in which I have specialised. An absurd and meaningless justification, for what value is there in guardianship for the period of your working life over that tiny corner of the world? So what if the particular corner that you have chosen (tax law perhaps, or orthopædic surgery) bestows on you a higher income than the average? Your life is no more valuable, you who watch the same television and eat food that, no matter how much more elaborately prepared, how much more expensive than your neighbour's, remains in essence the same. For life to be of value we must resist this dependence on others, this childish satisfaction in others' dependence upon us. If I have difficulty in obtaining gainful employment, such is a small price to pay for my liberation.

Yet I do need the money. I am not nor will ever be truly free. Why is it that I still feel this is a battle I might have won, when surely it was lost centuries ago?

At least I succeeded in giving the boy homework before I left. Vocabulary for the first conjugation and first declension. Every word to be memorised by the next lesson. He protested at having to work over the weekend, but I held firm. The boy will drift if left to his own devices. I must establish a framework for learning, and hope that he catches the feel of the language and becomes interested of his own accord, before he gives up in despair.

When the Chinappas came to the house to collect Mercy on their way to the boat that would take them all out of harm's way, safe and sound to Colombo, the sky was overcast, filled with dark brooding clouds that seemed to jostle one another in their rush to obscure the sun. The trunk had been sent on ahead. Father had said we should not go down to the docks. In recent days, when other ships had sailed, there had been a crush of people at the dockside, pushing, shoving, hoping that by some miracle they would find a berth, to anywhere, anyhow, so long as they could escape the Japanese demons.

But Mercy was not happy at being abandoned, here, at the door of her own home, not even escorted by her family to the ship. Her face darker even than the sky, she refused to talk to me, and, when Mother and Father in turn hugged her to them, her arms remained by her sides.

Although unsettled by Mercy's behaviour and assailed by an unease the source of which I still cannot fathom, I was nonetheless more anxious about Rose. It seemed fundamentally important to say goodbye to her properly, to elicit from her some gesture of affection that I could hold in my memory when we were apart. We stood together in one corner of the verandah. I remember moistening my lips with my tongue and then speaking to her in a soft, low voice.

"I will miss you, Rose."

"Don't be silly, Abraham. We'll be back soon. I expect the Nips will be stopped soon, maybe before Kuala Lumpur."

"I will miss you anyway."

Rose reached out a hand.

"You are silly. Please be careful. Be brave but don't be foolish."

There must be something else I could say, something she would remember across the miles. I had to find the words, and find them at once. She paused a moment, her smile a little quizzical, as if she too expected something more. My mouth opened, then closed. How foolish I must have looked, like a carp bumping up against the glass sides of a fish tank.

Then she was gone, turning to rejoin her family. I stood there watching till they were out of sight, the thought that any gesture must be inadequate, must seem too frivolous, keeping my arms frozen by my side.

"It's good that you are packed, son. In any case, unless those people are stopped, you and I will go to Lim Chu Kang. There is a small farm there. Appa says there may be more bombing in the city, and that it is too risky to stay here. He wants us to travel tomorrow."

"And Appa?"

"He will stay here. When it is safe he will come, or send word to us."

I walked slowly back up the driveway to the house, my shoes scuffing on the gravel, until Mother started scolding. I remember disappearing into my room and shutting the door, unable to talk to my parents as Rose slipped away. I sat on the edge of my bed and stared out through the dirty window pane. Rain began to fall, a sudden rush of water that drummed against the glass. Momentarily it seemed that the water was washing away dirt. But then (and this was a moment that has come back to me many times across the years, whenever I watch from indoors the start of a thunderstorm) I realised that all that was happening was the replacement of old dirt with new. The fragments of leaves, soil and dead insects that littered the outer sill of the window were being brought to life, made to dance, by the pounding rain. They jumped up against the window pane, smearing it anew. The rain's futility brought a strange comfort to me, then and each time I remember it. If I had lacked the courage to speak to Rose as my heart urged and as the moment demanded, and if it was then that I lost Rose — well, that was the way of things.

I remember too that as the rain consoled me I was overtaken by a giddy excitement. Rose might be leaving, but there was war looming on my doorstep. I half-regretted banishment to Lim Chu Kang, for if there was to be more bombing I wanted to see it. Perhaps I would distinguish myself by my bravery. Perhaps by the time Rose returned I would be acknowledged as a hero and given a medal to wear upon my chest. To see opportunity in danger, to seek out proofs of one's courage and strength: such is the vanity of youth. Surely to have survived this far, to have managed as well as I have done, surely that is achievement enough? Why then the prick of these recurring memories, why this disturbance of what should be a tranquil old age? Don't I deserve a rest, Mercy, won't I join you soon enough? I am not at fault, for you to haunt me so.

Six

*I*n Lim Chu Kang I made two discoveries. I learned that smelling funny did not make Chinese people any less decent or kind than ourselves, and that working with one's hands did not make one any less a human being. It was not that my parents had ever openly espoused propositions to the contrary, but somehow such had been the assumptions upon which my childhood was founded.

The farmer and his wife were hardly distinguishable one from the other, any differences having been weathered and eroded by years of exposure to the sun. Their three daughters, who giggled whenever they saw me, walked to school every day. Theirs was a Mandarin school, so even with them I could communicate only by means of simple Malay. Their textbooks took pride of place in the main room of the house. One entire shelf was reserved for them.

There was an altar outside the house. Mother, I am sure, kept her eyes averted from it, wary of heathen infection, but I was fascinated by its gaudy red paint, by the burning joss sticks and the offerings of fruit and rice. Beyond the cemented compound were a chicken coop, a well and the toilet outhouse. A large earthen jar collected rainwater for bathing. Past them were the undulating fields of vegetables: long beans, tomatoes, kai lan and others whose names I no longer recall. Clustered above them, at the top of the hill, were fruit trees: durian, jackfruit, guava and rambutan. I remember one afternoon eating guava until I was sick. My retching produced little more than an acidic bile, and the discomfort lasted into the night. An early lesson in the advantages of temperance.

Another day, as I was walking back after an afternoon's roaming, the sun already setting, I spotted the middle daughter proceeding to the earthen jar for her bath. Quickly I ducked behind a bush and watched her pour a scoopful of water over her shoulders and commence soaping. Of course she did not remove the cotton wrap she had about her, but as she progressed it clung ever more closely to her curves. A wicked excitement gripped me, as I sat there seeing but unseen. Joy mingled with shame in my release, the moment broken by my mother's voice calling for me. I scrambled back to the house by a roundabout route that I hoped would not compromise my hideout. Later that evening I shook my head in innocent denial when the girl, smiling all the while, wagged her finger at me. I wonder why I felt unable to express to her the desire that she had kindled in me, why I have always desired more than I have acted. Moderation perhaps, an understanding that restraint is a virtue.

Mother spent most of the days tut-tutting at the household arrangements. The cooking she held in particular scorn, and would mutter to me about the crying shame of it all when garlic was chopped finely and fried until charred. "Burnt like that it's very bitter," she would say without fail each mealtime. I, however, was fascinated: the great iron wok, black as night; the intense heat of the fire; and the rush and roar of ingredients as they were stirred in. Everything was faster and hotter than at home, where curries would bubble over a low flame for hours. There was a sense of vigour, of brusque impatience, that made our kitchen, and us in consequence, seem idle and slothful.

Richard's kitchen must be like that. All fervour and hurry. They have a maid from the Philippines, for whom the robust haste of Chinese cooking must be quite unnatural. He has decided to continue with his Latin lessons during the Christmas holidays, and, perhaps with more time to study, has begun to make surprisingly good progress. The important thing is to catch his interest, to show him how Latin can unlock a door through which one can glimpse the underlying pattern of the English language.

Another key to sparking the boy's enthusiasm is to start him on the translation of sentences that are no longer reminiscent of baby-talk, or, better still, on short prose passages.

Yesterday I gave him a description of a battle from Julius Cæsar's account of his conquest of Gaul. Cæsar's Latin is simple, intended for the widest readership, and so this passage, save for one or two sentence constructions simplified for beginners, was almost intact. I could see how the passage interested him with all its talk of phalanxes and carapaces, and the satisfaction he obtained from being able to manage most of the passage with minimal assistance was quite apparent. Seeing this tempted me into indulgence. I lost myself in reminiscences that can only have bored the boy.

"Reading about battles and foreign conquests also brings to my mind the dark days of the Occupation. I was about your age — no, perhaps a year older — when the Japanese came. That's something, isn't it?"

Richard's curiosity seemed to have been aroused, as well as a measure of disbelief, as if he was trying to picture me at his age, and managing only a vision of my worn and wrinkled face on the body of a young boy.

"What was it like?"

Embarrassment brought me to my feet. "I should be going, I suppose."

"Tell me about it."

I had started, and could hardly refuse such an earnest request. I sat down again.

"There's not much to tell, Richard. I didn't have any grand adventures you know." Frankly, I was busily searching my mind for exactly that — some grand adventure to impress the youth. "When the Japanese captured Singapore it was just me and my parents. My sister had gone by ship to Colombo, several weeks before the Japanese reached Johore. It was a good thing she left then, and not later, because many of the later transports were sunk, you see, because people in their desperation resorted to the most unseaworthy of vessels ... and enemy action too, that got worse. ... You know Colombo, I suppose, where it is?"

"Sri Lanka, capital," he murmured.

"My father packed my mother and me off to the countryside, Lim Chu Kang. It really was country then. We stayed on a farm. My father wouldn't let us stay in town because of the bombing ..."

The boy's face momentarily convulsed, as if I had said something funny. Unable to fathom what that might be, I was overtaken by an uneasy feeling that anything I might say must seem the ramblings of an old man. Was I just prattling on for his mocking amusement? My words quickened in my anxiety to finish the story and take my leave.

"My father stayed in town. He was working at the hospital, the General Hospital. As a senior clerk in the hospital administration. We stayed on this farm for what seemed like months. Father visited us once a week, driving out with a friend who owned a car, or else borrowing a hospital vehicle. We didn't get much news except from him. We could hardly communicate with the farmer and his family, or their neighbours. They all spoke dialect, hardly any

Malay, and certainly no English or Tamil. But it was fun. No school. And there was so much to explore: the chicken coop, the fields of vegetables and then beyond them the fruit trees, and rows and rows of rubber trees. But as the weeks went by there was more bombing ..." Another convulsion. The beginnings of a giggle. "... in town, and gunfire in the distance, until suddenly all was quiet. Not a sound. Only the cockerel kept up his crowing. After two days of quiet, we were desperate to find out what had happened. Who had won? Right up until the last moment we hoped for a miracle, for the Japanese to be turned back. Then, one morning, when I was watching that cockerel bossing his hens around as he must have done every day of his adult life, quite oblivious to the fact that the world was at war, I saw Father, walking up the road towards us. He had walked all the way — can you imagine? — more than six hours' walk, from the city. He must have started walking a few hours before dawn ... and when he reached us he, even he, my father, was tired out. He walked past me, hardly seeming to notice me, straight into the farmhouse in search of Mother. And when he saw her he sank right down into the nearest chair, flopped over like a sack of rice."

"Why did he have to walk?"

"The Japanese had straightaway taken over the hospital. And they were commandeering every vehicle they could find. They'd come down the Peninsula, all that way, many on bicycle or foot, and I imagine they thought it was someone else's turn to walk. Anyway, he told us to stay there (though we could hardly go anywhere else) until he could send us word that it was safe to return ... and of course we needed transport. Even a bullock cart would be better than Mother and me walking. He walked back, that same day, in the afternoon, after lunch, and after talking to the farmer, in a mixture of dialect and Malay. The farmer had been a patient at the hospital or something — I can't quite remember how my father had found him."

"But how were the Japanese?"

"One learned to get along with them. To bow and scrape at the appropriate times. My father was useful to them, as a hospital administrator, and they never touched him or any of my family. But he did no more than the bare minimum. He did not like or respect them. Fear them, of course, everyone feared them. But all he did was keep working, keep doing his job. He did not raise money for them from the Jaffna community or anything like that. I stopped school after picking up enough Japanese to work as a translator. My father told me to stop, because the Japanese took over the schools and he was sure they would not last."

"You knew that right from the beginning?"

"Father did. Somehow he always knew things. Others thought the British had been beaten far too soundly ever to return. The Americans too — they were torn to pieces at Pearl Harbour and in the Philippines. It wasn't that he doubted the strength of the Japanese. For many years he had warned that a war was coming. The Japanese were too strong to let Britain and America dominate the Pacific. He knew they were a powerful country. He knew too that they were brutal and would do anything to win. He visited the POW camps, with medical supplies when there were any, and he saw the POWs wasting away, while Japanese officers strutted around in smart uniforms. … No, his belief that the Japanese would not last long came from something much simpler — how could Japanese domination of the world be God's will? The Japanese brought nothing to Singapore but their guns. They despised the Malays, although they treated them best of all. The Chinese — how they hated the Chinese … for everything that a Japanese person thinks makes him special, better than the rest of the world, comes from China. That sense of inferiority made them especially brutal towards the Chinese. As for Indians, they wanted to use us against the British. They dreamed of rebellion against the Crown in India. Nor did they secretly despise us, as they did the Malays. They knew we could work hard and that the Buddhist part of what they call their religion came from India. … But they did have a horror of our skin. Our colour. Father had seen Japanese people steeling themselves before submitting to treatment, to being touched, by an Indian doctor. Now, what was I saying?"

"How your father was sure the Japanese would not win in the end."

"Oh yes, of course. The British had brought God's word and a system of law that protected all, regardless of race. The British thought their civilisation was best, but at least wanted to share it, you understand? The Japanese were even more convinced of their superiority, so much so that they believed their superiority was inherent in their race and could not be exported to other, inferior peoples."

I stopped at this point, my breathing heavy. I had lost my bearings somewhere in the course of my monologue. Was this what Father had thought or what I now believed? Father so rarely spoke at any length of his thoughts or feelings. I was putting words into his mouth. And why was I unburdening myself to this boy? I should have resisted his probing. Memories are elusive creatures, like butterflies. The more one tries to capture them, to put them on display, the more tangled one becomes in the net of one's remembrance.

"Do you mean the Japanese lost simply because they did not win over the people they conquered?"

"You're right. In Singapore they didn't. Or the Philippines. They did to some extent in Indonesia, where some people thought the Japanese were an improvement on the Dutch. But I'm saying a little more than that." Suddenly convinced once again of the truth of my words, remembering less the dark days of the Occupation than the bright years of my twenties, when Singapore was surging forward upon the tide of *Merdeka,* my voice strengthened. "Ideas count, not just force. I knew that Britain would win in the end because they had better ideas, however imperfectly they practised them."

"You mean Christianity must triumph ... democracy must win?"

Was the boy mocking me? A moment earlier I had been so sure of my insight, claiming it for myself rather than Father. Yet stated like that, as a universal law, it sounded absurd. The Bible certainly does not promise the triumph of right over might, not in this world. Only in heaven will the sins of the world be judged and condemned.

"I don't know, boy. Maybe not." My voice subsided to a whisper. I took my glasses off and, to conceal my confusion, massaged the bridge of my nose and rubbed my eyes.

"What about collaborators? Did you know any?"

I was relieved at the question, for it turned the conversation away from the theory that I had propounded and had come to doubt. I put my glasses back on and focused my gaze firmly upon Richard, only to be nonplussed by the intensity of his interest. "Of course. There were so many ..." I lost my train of thought for a moment, but then it came back to me, the face of Selvam, soft and pliable like latex, no doubt the product of the poisonous sap that ran in his veins. "This family who were our friends, their eldest son worked for the *Kempeitai.* What power he wielded! What fear he commanded! Oh, yes ... what an empire he built for himself, extorting money — no, he was cleverer, he extorted only durable valuables, jewellery, things like that, and how many followers he had … really a king. But of course, the fortunes of war changed. You have read the history?"

"Yes."

"How the British held onto Burma, and then the Japanese navy was destroyed by the American bombers?"

"Yes, at Midway?"

"That's right. So this gentleman had to start singing a different tune. Tried to use his influence to help people rather than rob them. But that wasn't easy. The clearer it became that the Japanese would not win, the meaner they got, and, as their lackey, he had to get meaner too."

"What happened when the British came back?"

"He disappeared. Went upcountry for many months. Then he came back, and with the money he'd made during the war, went to England to study law. He became a very successful lawyer."

"Didn't he get put on trial or anything?"

"No. Perhaps he didn't deserve any punishment. Perhaps I'm too hard on him. Maybe he had to do what he did. Or maybe …"

"Yes?"

"Maybe it is too much to expect justice in the world." This thought, contradictory to that of a few moments before, had triumphed. "Man is fallen. Why should it surprise us that the wicked and the unjust succeed where the pure of heart fail? Only in heaven will justice be done."

Seven

I see Victor once a week or so. He makes a point of treating me to a meal, the dutiful son. His apartment parades his youthful prosperity. This unsettles me. I am forced to sit on the edge of one of his large armchairs, for fear that I may otherwise sink into its depths, never to re-emerge. I prefer a straight-backed chair, such as he has in the dining room, but today I have decided against fuss.

I am irritated that Victor is fetching me a soft drink. Where is the wife who should take care of such things? Thirty-three and still not married. Of course courtship is different these days. I cannot interfere; that would only cause resentment. Still, there never seems to be a woman around, no one more than a friend. My son works too hard. It really is not healthy. Somehow the human race has trapped itself into accepting an ever faster pace of life. Twenty years ago no one worked beyond normal office hours. Nowadays Victor describes what he calls 'pulling an all-nighter' with an utterly absurd pride.

Perhaps my real concern is for myself. I'm sixty-eight and the burden of my years seems to weigh ever more heavily upon me. Father, born at the turn of the century, died in his mid-sixties, only a few years after Victor's birth, a few months after a stroke had left his right side paralysed. A desire to see grandchildren aches within me, to watch them pass the threshold that separates infant from child, so that they may carry me in their memories for the rest of their lives.

As Victor hands me my glass of ginger beer, I am struck by the paunch spreading across his middle and the cheeks unshaven because it's Sunday (a habit he did not inherit from me). With his hair thinning on top the boy looks practically middle-aged. Is he deliberately not marrying in order to spite his father? Abandoning his body to a lawyerly middle age in order to mock me, to mock those days when we played badminton or cricket together?

Of course it may just be a required attribute of the successful lawyer. A junior partner in a substantial law firm, a firm of good repute. Very few can climb so far, so fast. The boy has often said how important it is for a lawyer, for whom seniority seems to count more than ability, to look old. He's wiser than his father too, for he abjures politics, saying one can be perfectly comfortable keeping within the bounds set by our rulers, and that there's no reason why anyone should risk his career, or worse, for the sake of more freedom than he would know what to do with. His circumspection has certainly paid dividends, for he has, at his young age, been able to afford a professional decorator to do up his apartment, located on the fringes of one of Singapore's best residential areas. It was the decorator who chose this absurd armchair, whose taste is reflected in the painting on the opposite wall, two squiggles of red and blue paint. That's the point though. This is not a home. It's a display of his arrival in the world. Only a woman in the house could make it a home.

Victor will take me out to dinner shortly. There is no question of a meal at home. His imported kitchen of oak cabinets and red-tiled countertop is used, I imagine, only for the making of coffee and toast in the mornings. After dinner, he will no doubt dutifully drive his father home.

"I'll just change my shirt, then we can leave."

He wanders off to the bedroom. The boy has often suggested that I come and stay, for after all there is a spare bedroom, but I have always refused. Surely it is undignified for a father to be dependent on his son, to live in his son's house. In any case, I would be an intruder, and a hindrance. I might hamper his efforts to find a wife. If only Rani were still alive! She would have found Victor a good Tamil girl by now, and persuaded him to meet her, get to know her, and in the end marry her.

Cousins and old friends often speak to me, including some with unmarried daughters, yet I have always declined their help. How can I ever broach this subject with Victor? "You, Father, you of all people counselling marriage?" But perhaps I should subdue this fear, show some courage (which after all no one can say I lack), and act now, soon, before more years slip away.

My reverie is broken by the ring of the telephone.

"Can you answer please?"

I pick up the receiver. "Hello."

"Hi Victor. Free this evening?" Something about the voice makes me uneasy.

"No. This is Victor's father. I'll ask him to come."

"Thanks, Mr Isaac, sir. Tell him it's Johnny."

I put down the receiver and call Victor to the phone.

"Hi, Johnny ... no, not this evening. ... I'll call you ... later ... ten, ten-thirty. ... Bye."

In the lift lobby I find myself asking questions.

"Who's Johnny?"

"A friend."

"I never heard of him before. Is he a lawyer?"

"No. He … he runs an art gallery."

"I don't like the way he sounds."

"Dad, he's a friend. Why should I care how he sounds?"

Victor's tone of voice puts a stop to any further questions. There are echoes of Mercy in that tone. How stubborn she was! Nothing could shake her from her resolve!

When she came back from Colombo, after the War ended, she was so quiet. She seemed never to speak. If she was not reading, then she was staring into space. When someone else spoke to her she would shut the speaker up before he had managed a complete sentence, adopting that same firm tone of voice that Victor had just employed.

She was like him in one other way too. She refused to marry. How Mother fretted and worried! How Father raged! But to both cajolery and anger Mercy remained impassive, as unmoved as a block of wood. She would sit there, her eyes locked in front of her, her hands on her knees, and say she would marry when she was good and ready, not a moment sooner.

No, it was not immediately after the War that she refused to marry. She could not have been older than eighteen or nineteen then. It was later, a few years later, perhaps only shortly before Rose set sail for London. At first our parents tolerated her silences. She had been separated from them for a number of years, important years for a young girl. Perhaps she felt a stranger, and needed time to get used to her family once again. But after a few years had passed, when it had become clear that Mercy had no enthusiasm for anything except her weekly trip to the public library, they began alternately to coax and nag her.

As for me, I could not complain that she was sharp or offensive. It was just that she kept her distance, so that I was never really sure what she was thinking. It's the same with Victor now. Why does the boy never confide in his father?

When we reach Victor's car I wave away my son's arm, but do, however, leave it to Victor to close the door.

"Where are we going to eat?"

"Would you like to have Thai food? A new restaurant just opened nearby."

"I don't understand all these new restaurants, all these new tastes. No wonder young people are so confused today. They don't grow up on a steady diet ... so they lack a clear reference point — Jaffna cooking, Cantonese, whatever. It's just a jumble ... Thai, French, hamburgers. No wonder everyone is so confused."

Victor smiles: an amused, tolerant and patronising smile. No one takes an old man seriously.

"OK. Thai food. But not too hot, please. My stomach can't take all those little chillies."

As I feared, the chillies did unsettle my stomach. In consequence, the night is punctuated by frequent trips to the toilet, undertaken in the dark and on tiptoe, for fear of waking the other occupants of the flat. The room is rented from a young South Indian couple. Their little girl sleeps in a cot in their room and if I wake her, her bawling will rouse her parents and keep all of us awake for the hour it will take to calm her. The effort of attempting sleep in the brief intervals between these hushed journeys soon exhausts me beyond the point where success remains possible. I try to occupy my mind so as to evade any excursion into the past. For a while I thumb listlessly through Augustine's *Confessions*, my stomach reproached by its call for men to turn their thoughts away from nature and nature's appetites. But the familiar words are strangely unsatisfying, as if for the first time I am realising that Augustine spoke to a different age, to men of a different cast of mind. Resigned to the inevitable, I succumb to the temptation to return once more to my trove of Rose's letters.

My dear Abraham,

I will be posting this letter at Aden tomorrow, together with another letter that I have already sealed. Thus, I write this letter, one might say, as a postscript.

Last night I lay awake, thinking about all of you at home. My thoughts, dear Abraham, turned especially towards Mercy. She is spirited, and stubborn, for knowledge of which qualities I must thank the time we spent together in Colombo. She proved herself very able in her studies there, and I was given to understand that the teacher of literature at the convent school had the highest regard for her.

I mention this, dear Abraham, because I am convinced that it would be a shame if she were not encouraged in her studies, or worse, discouraged or prevented from their continuance. I remember that you told me that she had not fussed, or shown any real anxiety, when your parents indicated that she had studied all she needed in order to become a good wife, but, Abraham, forgive me, you must learn that people, especially women, do not always express how they feel.

Forgive me once again, Abraham, if I seem to be interfering, but Mercy and you are sister and brother to me. You told me of that incident with the tea, and I have thought upon it over these past few days. Abraham, if your parents are unable to understand, well, then you must, and you must make them understand.

There, I have said what I wanted to say. Take these words, please, only as I have intended them, as words from your loving sister.

May the Almighty bless you and guide you.

Yours ever,

Rose

My hand trembles as I put the letter down. For a moment the paper trembles too, rustling against a stack of books. Loving sister. Her brother. I stand up and walk to the window. The room is in a three-room Housing and Development Board flat, on the tenth floor of a block that stands among hundreds like it in this new town of Toa Payoh and elsewhere across the island. What happened to the old neighbourhoods, the houses, streets and fields that hugged the curves and folds of the earth? How have I ended up here, standing in one concrete box among thousands identical to it, my position within the grid of Singapore fixed by the coordinates of street, block and apartment number? And where is Rose now, where in that green and pleasant land? And Mercy? Her face appears for a moment, lips set firmly, head held high on an upright neck, and then it disappears, back into the shadows cast by the reading lamp.

I moved in here about two years ago, shortly after the couple were married. The boy's parents have left Singapore to retire to India, where no doubt they must live comfortably, on the father's savings and pension from the Malayan Railway. The girl's parents live with one of her brothers, in one of the newer housing estates … Tampines, I think; somewhere in the east at any rate.

My room faces the common corridor that runs the length of the block, providing access to all the flats. The window is divided vertically by iron bars and horizontally by aluminium shutters. The shutters are open, and peering through them I can see the brick and concrete wall of the adjacent block, some thirty metres distant. From here I can see neither ground nor sky; for a view of either I must leave the room and stand outside in the common corridor.

I keep to myself, to this room. The girl frequently offers food, which I only accept when the demands of politeness forbid otherwise. It is only on Deepavali, for a special meal, that I cannot avoid joining them. Frankly, I am not sure that they are all that clean, least of all in the preparation of food.

Suddenly I remember that I have switched on the electric heating coil to boil water in an enamel mug for tea. A hope that it may quiet my stomach, or at least expedite the clearing of my system must have motivated me. The water's been boiling for some minutes now, and I hurry to switch off the element at the mains. I pour some of the hot water over a tea bag placed in a cup. Victor introduced me to tea bags. I wonder now how I ever had the patience to deal with loose tea leaves. Yet even though I am grateful for their convenience, I am saddened by the thought that this incessant striving for the easiest way to do things, though no doubt the engine of progress for society, must inevitably weaken us, make us less and less capable as individuals, and moreover that this convenience goes hand in hand with the decline of the family. Which is cause and which effect? Do teabags, by reducing dependence on wife or mother, hasten the family's break-up, or is it merely that the break-up of the family has unleashed a demand for an easier way to make tea? Rose's words come to mind. She even urged me to take action of some sort or other, but didn't I always do everything possible for my sister? Didn't I?

How angered I was by Mercy's behaviour that day! There we were entertaining Mercy's first suitor, all of us, and especially me, on best behaviour, and she had let us all down, and herself too. Mother's sister had made contact through one of her own friends with a good Jaffna Tamil family, Methodists, who lived in Johore, across the Causeway. Their son, having entered the priesthood and taken charge of his first parish, was in search of a good Christian wife. We were Anglican, but that was no real barrier. We were not Catholics or Hindus, and that was all that really mattered. Mercy was perfect for his requirements, for she had sufficient education to be a valuable support to him in his parish. He for his part seemed to our parents to be close to ideal: not only a man of God, but one already entrusted with his own parish, and so financially secure and with a promising future.

It was a Saturday afternoon, but I was dressed in my Sunday best. Mother had spent the previous day making a number of delicious sweetmeats, the responsibility for the best of which would be quietly, but firmly, attributed to Mercy.

Mercy had been taken by Mother a few days before to find a new length of material for a sari, and, immediately after a light lunch on that momentous day, Mother began to fuss and toil over her daughter's appearance: oiling and plaiting her hair, helping her to apply her make-up and, later, adjusting her sari. Father wandered in and out, complaining that the man was a priest, for God's sake, surely he wouldn't be interested in the girl's appearance. Mother of course knew better, and, exasperated by what she called his nonsense, eventually shooed him out of the room, and forbade him further entry.

While I accepted that the first visit of a suitor and his family was a matter entirely within Mother's responsibility and expertise, I nonetheless felt that she was overdoing things. A family can only

61

assist in bringing together a daughter and a prospective husband: surely the rest is up to the two individuals. Mercy, I could see, was a little overwhelmed by the occasion, and I was sure that the reason for her silence and her fixed smile (the determined expression of someone undergoing, and desperate to survive, an exhausting test of endurance) was fear, a fear induced by Mother's apparent belief in the overriding importance of this first meeting. As she dressed and coiffed Mercy, she chattered on about her visit with Father to Johore Bahru the previous week, when they had met with the young priest's family. What a handsome man he was, how confident of manner and polished of speech! On and on went Mother's patter, rambling from one fine quality to the next. No wonder Mercy was overawed. She had been made nervous to an extreme, and that, combined with her natural clumsiness, must have been the cause of what happened. It had not been a sign of anything else, not a portent of things to come. Rose had presumed too much, and I was never guilty, most certainly not, of any sin of omission.

At last they had arrived, fifteen minutes after the time agreed upon. The parents entered first: the father in a dark suit, his face solemn and his step measured; the mother, by contrast, in a red sari, her face eager and her eyes darting quickly around the room, no doubt noting the cane furniture, the grandfather clock and the wooden General Electric radio. Then came the go-between, our aunt's friend, white-haired, yet her step light and brisk as if buoyed up by her triumph in bringing these two families together. Bringing up the rear was the young man himself, but I immediately realised that he had hung back, not from shyness, but rather from a desire to emphasise his nonchalance about the present proceedings. His priestly collar was displayed beneath a proudly uptilted chin.

Father and I greeted them all, and asked them to take a seat. Mercy and Mother were of course not present yet: they were still in the kitchen making tea to bring in together with the sweetmeats.

How resentful I felt, sitting stiffly in my chair, of the scrutiny I was receiving. I lacked the confidence to return that scrutiny, to meet that young priest's gaze with my own, or run my eyes over him, to check in my turn the other's posture and dress. Father talked, polite enquiries as to health and the pleasantness of the journey, until Mother entered, followed by Mercy. Mercy did not look at the assembled company. Her eyes remained demurely downcast. The young priest made no more than a vague movement, the merest hint of getting to his feet, when Mercy was introduced to him. He settled back into his chair, his legs crossed as if he were a buyer in an auction awaiting an appropriate moment to enter the bidding. His eyes wandered over Mercy as she bent down to place the tray of teacups on the low table in the centre of the room.

Mercy served the father, the mother and the friend before serving the young priest. I am convinced that, as she walked towards the man, their eyes met. I remember well the look of that young man, a mixture of the anxiety brought on by lust and of the triumph caused by the certainty that his lust, if he so wished it, would be satisfied, all in good time. I remember the anger that sent blood rushing to my ears, so that what happened next seemed to take place at a great distance. Mercy, as if halted by the young man's stare, paused momentarily, and then the tea cup appeared to take on a life of its own, to jump from her hand and fall, slowly, towards the young man's lap, the hot brown liquid outpacing the falling cup, exploding into his crotch, while the cup fell onto the chair between his legs, bouncing and falling without breaking onto the terrazzo floor.

I remember standing up, as if trying to catch that cup before it fell, as the room went deathly quiet, the only sound the blood pounding in my ears. Then the young man screamed, shouting at Mercy. It was an accident, surely, the girl was nervous, and Mother ran to the priest's side, apologies pouring from her lips, trying at one and the same time to quiet him and to rouse him to follow her to the bathroom, where the spill could be quickly and efficiently dealt with. The young man was responding, the shock and pain had only been momentary, everything was going to be all right. He was beginning to get to his feet, when I heard the sound, a gurgle that started in Mercy's throat, growing into something else as her mouth opened, growing into a roar that seemed to shake the windows.

The cup of tea has gone cold in my hands. That scene is as vivid as if it were being re-enacted now, here in this tiny garret. The young man shaking off Mother, standing up and brushing roughly past Mercy towards the door. His parents following, grim-faced: the mother waving her hands, as if protecting her son from my sister; the father stern, but his pace quickening as he strode towards the door. None of them looked back, as if mindful of the fate of Lot's wife. The friend, however, appeared unable to tear her gaze from this personification of Sodom and Gomorrah: she left the room backwards, staring at Mercy, from whom, in fierce bursts, rattled the machine gun of her laughter.

Eight

Mercy's spilling of the tea was the talk of the town, or so it seemed at the time. The self-importance of youth. The world ignores our antics rather more than we wish to believe. It was not just myself, however. My parents felt their humiliation keenly, and this fuelled a fierce anger towards Mercy. Mother scolded and nagged. Father was less voluble, but his exasperation at Mercy's conduct was no less visible. I was dismayed by her behaviour, and confronted her that same evening, in her room, to which our parents had ordered her.

"How could you do this? Why did you agree to meet him in the first place?"

"Was I asked?"

"You could have said no."

"Appa and Amma just want to be rid of me, to marry me off."

Mercy was seated on the bed. I stood over her.

"That is so unfair. They want what's best for you. They took a lot of trouble."

"Yes, of course. Enough, Annai. Your words are just the gibbering of a monkey."

A spasm of anger shook me. My fists clenched, but I resisted the urge to strike her.

In the days that followed, Mercy slipped from my mind. Rose, as ever, ousted all else. The next day, as I recall, we arranged to meet at the Adelphi Cafe. That day she told me what I had long dreaded to hear.

"Charles and I are to be married."

"Rose ..." I was silenced by a sudden rush of hatred for that pale man, whose complexion was dirtied by a thousand freckles. How confidently Charles had captured Rose, made her his possession. My eyes closed as I struggled to clear my mind. Rose's voice was so cheerful, so sure that I would share her joy. Should I say something to her, or hold my peace, even though this must be my last opportunity? When I opened my eyes her smile had frozen into puzzlement. "Rose ..." I tried again.

Her hand reached across the table and grasped my arm.

"Say nothing." And then she took back her hand and, her eyes shining in the reflected light of a happy future, told me of their plans, to marry and live in England, for Charles to return to the English Bar. I heard but did not listen, regretting already my obedience to her command, obedience born of habit, knowing that this second chance to speak had passed, and that it was almost certainly my last.

I did not go to see Rose off, pleading classes at the Teachers' College. Our goodbye, at the Chinappas' house on the eve of her departure, was stiff and formal, even though Charles was not present. The nights that followed were restless ones, my mind wandering to Rose, her voice soaring from the choir stalls opposite, that narrow gulf of nave widening with the ocean over which Rose's liner now voyaged. Yet in time she sank from my conscious mind, as I concentrated on learning in order to teach. Submerged in my subconscious, she was like a rock on which my thoughts would suddenly founder when I least expected, its sharp edges tearing at my composure.

Through one of the part-time tutors at the College I found an opening for Mercy to teach English at a primary school, a post for which a teaching diploma was not required. To both my surprise and my parents', Mercy accepted the position. Father, initially a little concerned that his daughter should postpone the sacrament of marriage for the base coin of employment, overcame his doubts when I reminded him that some time would undoubtedly pass before another suitor dared venture up our driveway.

Mercy seemed to grow with her new-found career. She ate better, as if storing energy for the next day's teaching. She took to wearing skirts, not every day, but once or twice a week, and quickly made friends in the staff room. With them she went shopping or even to the cinema. One day I bumped into her, in town, together with a Chinese lady whose slim figure had drawn my attention before I recognised my sister. The two of them were smoking, their chatter punctuated by laughter. As Mercy introduced me I tried somehow to combine a friendly smile for her companion with a disapproving frown at Mercy's cigarette. Mercy must have been struck by the contortions of my face, for she kept giggling throughout the introduction, so that anger at her chased away the pleasantries that had begun to form in my mind. They excused themselves and walked away once it became apparent that I had little to offer by way of conversation.

As the months passed however, our parents' thoughts turned back to the search for a husband for Mercy. To Mother especially, the fear that Mercy might never marry had become a burden that literally seemed to weigh upon her, so that she had begun to stoop and her sari to hang loose upon her listless frame. I gathered up my courage and told Father that it was essential for the matter to be discussed fully with Mercy. I endeavoured to explain that a young woman of Mercy's temperament might not see marriage and children as the only goal of her life. Father exploded at the uttering of such atheistic blasphemies, calling me a Communist like those black-and-whites, before subsiding, his head resting on his arms. A few moments later, he roused himself and, shaking his head in disgust at the modern world, agreed that Mercy would of course be consulted.

So one evening, after the dinner plates had been cleared away, the four of us sat back down at the dining table. To my surprise, Mercy sat calm and still as Father spoke of their plans once again to seek a husband for her.

"I am sure I need not explain to you the benefits of having someone who will provide for you when we are gone. And children, Mercy. To marry is to serve the Lord's purpose."

Mercy smiled. "I can always provide for myself, Appa, and I'm sure St Paul would disagree with you about marriage, but really as long as the man's modern-minded, I will not protest."

Mother looked at her, her voice weary. "And you promise no more of the old nonsense."

"Oh that," Mercy's voice was light and melodious. "That was an accident. I just couldn't help laughing, everyone was so serious." And she laughed, a gay tinkle.

So Mercy was married, to a young, newly qualified doctor whom Father knew personally and approved because he worked hard at the hospital, whom Mother endorsed once she had checked his background, and whom Mercy liked, for doctors were by the nature of their profession modern, and David, for he bore that good and honest name, appeared gentle and attentive to her, while not without a sense of humour. After the initial meeting, they went out alone a few times, and, said Mercy to my horror one evening, she had tested her smoking on him. "He's not like you, you old man in boy's clothing … he smokes himself."

At the wedding I assisted the young doctor, in fact assumed the duties of best man. In that capacity I quickly learned to respect David's confidence and the calm way in which he dealt with the planning of the wedding and the reception. Father gave Mercy away. His face was grave yet his eyes beamed contradiction to the firm set of his mouth as he steered her slowly up the aisle, bathed in the warm, applauding gaze of friends and relatives. Mother could not stop crying, even after the service was over and we were at the reception in the church hall.

Mercy turned to me and said, "She's crying more today than when I left for Colombo, when she might never have seen me again."

"Marriage means the loss of her daughter," I replied, regretting my glib words as Mercy's lips froze, fixed in the outline of the smile that a moment before had animated them.

David, taking advantage of a pause in the number of people who wished to shake his hand, leaned over.

"She's lost into safe hands, that's for sure." He put his arm around Mercy's waist. "I hope you're ready to be an uncle." He winked at me, while I wondered why the blood had fled from my sister's lips.

Nine

*I*nvited to the Yeos' cocktail party in the week before Christmas, I find their house transformed. It is filled with people, friends and business associates presumably. I am terrified by all these beautiful, rich and self-assured individuals, and regret accepting the mother's invitation. She was probably as surprised as I was when I said how pleased I would be to come. And why have they invited me? What have I to offer them? Or, since after all this is the season of giving, is it intended as a form of bonus, to give me the chance to eat and drink well?

Stepping into the house, I can see that it has been thoroughly scrubbed, carpets vacuumed and beaten, marble floors polished and furniture waxed. The contents of the crystal decanters on the bar, whisky, brandy and sherry, sparkle through the cut glass. I feel like wandering around on a tour of inspection, for I am really quite heartened to find that I am perhaps not alone in my trepidation at these social occasions. For the Yeos to put in so much effort they too must be nervous, anxious to make the right impression. Of course not to impress me, to imagine such a thing would be folly, a false gratification, but nonetheless the reminder that there are others of whom even the Yeos must be in awe is strangely encouraging. Catching sight of the row of Indian silver elephants (bull, cow and three calves of various sizes) that adorn the sideboard, I have to resist the temptation to walk across and find out if I can see my teeth, my dentures, reflected in their curved surfaces.

In the back garden stands a large canvas tent, its stark outlines only slightly softened by baskets of hanging flowers. Although it is not raining, I am impressed by their foresight, their decision not to leave the comfort of their guests, too numerous to be satisfactorily accommodated within the confines of the house, to the vagaries of Providence. There is a bar at one end of the tent, staffed by waiters in white jackets that seem to be one size too small. Some of them circulate among the guests, taking orders for drinks, or handing round trays of titbits, multi-hued arrangements upon little roundels of bread. I think of Katong, of those seaside bungalows, the bee-hives and slit skirts of the tycoons' mistresses, all those parties to which I and those of my ilk were never invited, and, thus moved, reach out and grasp one of these variegated morsels. It looks better than it tastes.

I take a drink off a tray, thinking it to be orange juice, and discover that it is in truth some sort of punch with a defi-nitely alcoholic kick. It has been a long time since I drank al-cohol, and for some reason I decide, in the spirit of festivity, to carry on breaking my long abstinence. I finish the first glass, and take another. Suitably charged and emboldened, I plunge into the mêlée, and soon realise that the apparent chaos dis-guises a careful ordering of the guests into dozens of discreet clusters.

I pause on the fringes of one such cluster, its members turning slightly towards me and throwing me quick, friendly glances until I am included in their conversation. This is easier than I expected. They seem genuinely interested in my teaching of Latin. I am a novelty perhaps amidst these captains of industry, tyros of politics. The pursuit of power has so plainly triumphed over intellectual

71

enquiry that I must seem a welcome change. I am at once the centre of attention, and seize the opportunity to reach out to these men of action, to grace their lives of toil and effort with a little speculatory enlightenment.

"The Romans transformed city state into empire on the backs of their warriors and merchants. Can we not do the same, minus perhaps the warriors? Can Singapore not aspire to the same or greater glory?"

There are murmurs of assent, exchanges of approving glances.

"Our problem, however, as the Romans soon came to realise, is that money and power are not everything, not even a good guarantee of more money, more power. That is the essential insight. As the Romans learned from the Greeks, acquired from them the accoutrements of civilization, so must we too learn, and not just from the West, from Britain, lately Great, but also from the grand old civilisations of Asia: India, China …"

Richard's mother appears and steers me to one side. I am delighted that she has singled me out. She looks resplendent in an off-the-shoulder ballgown with puffy sleeves, a shimmering green fabric. She looks like Imelda Marcos, and I tell her so.

"Mr Isaac, Richard is along here. Let me take you to him."

As she pulls me along with her she turns to me momentarily and says the punch is rather strong, don't I think? All the better for it, I say, raising my glass and smiling at any ladies that we pass. So this is how the well-to-do spend their evenings. How splendid. This is what I missed, all those years ago in Katong.

Ah, there's Richard. He's engrossed by some pompous, red-faced fellow who's pontificating upon some ponderous subject or other. I say hello to him, we exchange a few pleasantries, and then find ourselves running out of conversation. In the silence of our pauses I hear the man waxing eloquent upon Western conspiracies against Asia, against the Chinese.

"Lau Teng Kee, Member of Parliament," Richard whispers.

Looking at the man, glass of no doubt Scotch whisky in his hand, I immediately conclude that he is one of those men in Government who believe themselves more important than they really are, but are never disabused of their inflated notions of themselves because they are nonetheless of some importance. Anyone of greater power and importance is never given the opportunity to take such men down a peg or two, because they always abase themselves in front of those with more power.

"Now, you have to understand the motives of the USA. You think they care about human rights? If you do you are naïve, a dupe. Here in East Asia at last we have got our acts together, doing business, making money, making things better and cheaper than the Americans. So of course what do the Americans do?"

The man pauses, looking slowly round the group. He smiles at Richard, and looks somewhat puzzledly towards me.

"Let me tell you. They stir things up. They try to rock the boat, so that we can't go faster than them. They turn students against teachers, workers against bosses and ..." He looks at the only woman among us, a smile forming at the corners of his mouth. "... women against men. Do you think they really care for the rights of students, workers or women? No way, as the Yanks say, no way. They just want to cause trouble for all the governments in the region, slow down our economies and keep the white man on top."

He looks round again, visibly gratified by the rapt, attentive faces. Richard appears fascinated by what the man has said. This irritates me, my pupil's mind captured by such drivel. I hesitate, stumbling over the words that I do eventually piece together.

"Aren't the Americans rich and democratic? Can't the two go together?"

The man laughs, a little nervously perhaps. He is unsure who I am, whether or not I may, in spite of my humble dress, be of some importance. He evidently concludes that I am not, and launches a counterattack.

"I should have thought the answer is obvious. We East Asians do things by consensus. We all agree on a goal and then don't waste any more time talking about it. So we can concentrate on achieving the goal. But the Americans want us to argue with one another so that we lose sight of the goal. Perhaps the gentleman is naïve, taken in by American propaganda."

"How do you know that we all agree on your goals, if you do not ask us first?"

The man looks visibly flustered, and I flush with my success. Perhaps I should after all have stood for Parliament. If this is the calibre of its denizens, why, I would have been a veritable star.

"Of course, my dear fellow, I'm not denying there shouldn't be consultation. It all depends on the circumstances, what sort of threats and dangers there are. In the old days, with the Communists knocking on the door, we had to be absolutely tough, resolute. Now of course the nation can afford a slightly more open style of government. We shall of course consult. All I'm saying is that unlike the Americans we know when to pull together, when to shut up for the sake of the common good, and just because Communism seems, and I repeat, seems, to have collapsed, doesn't mean there are no more threats. I think America is a potential threat, because it is they who are scared, scared of us. They would like nothing better than for us to descend into anarchy or chaos, like ..." And here he pauses, as if to make sure that I am listening. "... like India, or one of those dark places in Africa."

I am incensed, but only for a moment. Then weariness descends upon me. To think that the future of my country lies in the hands of men like this, of the narrowest parochialism, the glibbest complacency. Is there no one who can articulate a future other than the superficially material, riding upon the growth of the nations around us, living off their energy, their endeavour, as we sip whisky in our secure little havens? Or will any such man inevitably be crushed, the immense machinery of government turned against him, while our citizens lower their heads and busy themselves, making money for the good of the nation, or else wining and dining prospective spouses in the pursuit of babies, another national duty in which I never excelled. In the end my reply is tangential, veering into irrelevance.

"I thought we supported the Americans. Didn't we support their bombers in Kuwait?"

"That's a different matter entirely. There they were defending our interests as well. It just so happened that our interests coincided. They're not white knights in shining armour, you know, these American bom-*bers* as you call them."

Suddenly everyone is laughing. I look around at their faces, reddened by alcohol into a florid harshness. I have spoken other than in their manner of speaking, betraying my upbringing, my Tamil otherness, most of all my insignificance. What are the words of a Latin teacher to those of a man of influence, a man with business to turn your way? How could the others not laugh at me? I turn to leave the party, keeping my head erect even as the room dissolves before me. Somehow, by some immense effort of will, I keep the path immediately before me in focus, keep my legs moving. It would not do to faint here, here in the midst of my enemies. Sliding door. The brightness of the living room. Hall and blessed exit beyond.

Open air, breeze upon my face and I am better. It is a long walk out to the main road. Looking back I see Richard, emerging from the doorway, his face in shadow. I cannot see his eyes, do they mock me, me his old teacher? I turn away, attempt to quicken my pace, and then he is beside me. The futility of an old man's haste! I scowl at him, and then see his concern.

"Mr Isaac, are you all right?"

"Go back, boy, of course. Time to leave."

"I thought you were going to get him. I don't think anyone's argued with him in ages. Mum calls him the man without a spine. Mum and Dad were at University with him. He was a real radical then, wanted to change the world ..."

"As you do, no doubt?" I curse the irony in my tone. The boy is sincere, and I, I can only mock.

"I'll never be like him."

I look at him now with new eyes, see the firm set of the jaw, the strong eyes that hold mine.

"I believe you," I say, and reach out a hand. The world is not yet lost, nor I with it.

Ten

Seated in Komala Vilas in Serangoon Road, to which I have come to salve my humiliation at last night's party, breaking off a piece of *vadai* to dip into the coconut chutney, a glass of sweet, hot tea in front of me, yet another teatime comes to mind, many years before, when *vadai* too was served. *Vadai* is probably my favourite teatime snack, and Mercy no doubt had sought that day to please me. At first I try to shrug off the association, to concentrate instead on the delicious contrast of crisp, deep-fried exterior and soft, doughy interior, my tongue mining unerringly the treasures of fried onion and green chilli buried within. Yet the *vadai* itself now seems to pull me irresistibly into this recess of my memory.

It was a few months after Mercy's wedding, that day when I was invited to tea at David's parents' house. It was there that the couple intended to stay, at least for the first few years of their marriage. The house stood in its own compound in a lane off Race Course Road, within walking distance of the bus stop on Serangoon Road where I alighted. Then, as now, this was the commercial heart of the Indian community, where spices, cooking pots, tiffin carriers and material for saris could be bought from dozens of stores all in fierce competition with one another. Walking here always thrills me, yet at the same time the crowds oppress me. When someone brushes against me, fear of contamination, in spite of myself, flies through me, as if I am unable to shake off the centuries of caste and tradition. I remember clearly once (that day perhaps?) passing a vendor of betel-nut sitting on the pavement, a row of filled green leaves arranged on the wooden tray in front of him. The memory is vivid: the vendor looking up at me, hopefully, deferentially, his red-stained mouth opening in respectful greeting. I strode on without a word.

When I reached the house I found it surrounded by a wall of about a man's height. The plaster was grey and crumbling, patchworked with green moss. The iron gates were shut, and a dog snarled menacingly from behind them, its brown coat ragged and diseased, revealing mottled pink skin where the fur was thinnest.

"David, Mercy," I called. The dog began barking and pushing at the gate.

A voice called from within, harsh words, directed at the dog, and then Mercy appeared, her face pale, except for dark rings around her eyes. She held a big clump of keys grasped tightly in her right hand, as if she were a prison warder admitting a visitor to the cells. She stepped down from the verandah towards the gates, shooing away the dog which growled even at her, and then opened them. I stepped inside, and nodded awkwardly at her, avoiding the traditional Tamil embrace for relatives: nose to cheek with a sharp inhalation of breath.

The front room was bare, except for a settee and two armchairs, thin cushions on a rattan frame and a low side table on which stood a glass vase filled with dusty plastic roses. The walls too were bare, except for a pendulum clock whose dull tick filled the room.

"Ginger beer or some tea?"

"Ginger beer will be fine. Don't trouble yourself."

"No trouble." She offered me a wan smile.

She disappeared into the back of the house, returning a few minutes later with a frosted glass filled with ginger beer and two small plates, one with a piece of fruitcake on it, the other with a *vadai*, a splash of chutney by its side.

"David was supposed to be back, but he may have to work late at the hospital."

I nodded, then, with a broad sweep of my arm to indicate the household, asked, "So how's married life?"

She smiled, her lips pressed thinly together, her eyes downcast. Then she looked up, her face solemn. "As good as could be expected, Annai. One must make adjustments."

"Yes, that's true." Impressed by her new-found practicality, I was searching for appropriate words of praise and approval when David's mother appeared at the doorway. I stood up to greet her. She enquired after my health, and when I replied that I was in general well, she retreated.

"David's mother is very nice."

Mercy looked at me again, her eyes widening. She seemed about to say something, then bit her words back, and only after that began to speak.

"Yes, she is ... only she likes things done her way."

I laughed. "Don't we all?" I took a mouthful of the *vadai*. It was cold, and had gone a little soggy.

"How are Appa and Amma?"

"Fine. When are you and David coming to visit?"

"I don't know. David is always so busy."

"You could drop by on your own."

"I don't think ..."

I had lifted the ginger beer to my mouth and seemed to miss the conclusion of her sentence. I put the glass down, and must for a moment have contemplated asking her to repeat her answer. But presumably her gaze was intent elsewhere, perhaps on some dusty spot that the servant had overlooked. Instead, having abandoned the *vadai*, I picked up the fruitcake, and, after first turning it over in my hands, began to chew on it slowly, fixing my attention on it.

"I've given up smoking."

"Good, good," I mumbled through a mouthful of the cake. My mind had wandered to a letter I was drafting, a letter to the Editor of *The Straits Times,* concerning self-government and the various racial communities in Singapore. I wished, having first set out my credentials as a member both of a racial and of a religious minority, to stress the importance of a unified political structure, one which would avoid divisions along racial lines. I had already formulated an opening sentence: 'If the maxim of imperial control is "divide and rule" then that of democratic self-government must be "unify and consult".'

"More ginger beer?"

I roused myself. "No, I've had plenty. I must, I suppose, be going."

She seemed disappointed that I was leaving so soon, but perhaps it was just that she was a little tired by the responsibilities of married life, responsibilities to which she was, in her own felicitous phrase, adjusting. She stood up and followed me to the gate. The dog ambled over from its place of repose, beneath the shade of a stunted rambutan tree, and sniffed my ankles. I withdrew them quickly, and a sharp word from Mercy made the dog retreat, its head cowed but teeth bared. I paused as she swung the gate open.

"God keep you in his care."

She made no reply, so I turned and strode off, not looking back, my mind returning to the argument of my letter, an argument which, in that age of new directions, of limitless possibilities, would make a difference.

In those days all seemed possible. Unlike my parents, I was thoroughly excited by the prospect of Independence. They had left

Ceylon and come to Singapore as administrators of Empire and were concerned that their welcome might not outlast the coming of self-rule. As they saw it, self-rule must mean in effect the rule of the majority, and who were the majority but the Chinese? From time to time Father talked of returning to Ceylon, but took no concrete steps towards that objective, nonetheless counselling caution, and detachment from political activities.

I became an active member of the Teachers' Union. I had no doubt that I, and other Tamils, could fully contribute to the shaping of Singapore's future. It was simple: the British had taught that all men were equal and therefore should participate, through political parties and elections, in the government of their nation. All one had to do was finally, after all these years, put British theory into practice. All sections of society should be free to voice their opinions. It was in this spirit that I drafted and submitted my letter to the Editor of *The Straits Times*.

Safely back in my room, I seek it out. That letter was a great triumph surely, something to weigh against all the rest.

The Editor
The Straits Times

Dear Sir

If the maxim of imperial control is 'divide and rule', that of self-government must be 'unify and consult'.

I speak, sir, as a gentleman proud of his Jaffna Tamil heritage, yet also respectful of the heritage of his neighbours, the Indian, the Chinese and the Malay, for in this island, or this Peninsula, we are fortunate in the rich and abundant diversity of our forebears.

81

In the debate on constitutional arrangements that must proceed henceforth with ever greater urgency as we speed towards the desideratum of self-government, I urge that we do not fall into the error of separate electoral rolls, nor into that of guaranteed representation of a particular community, whether by appointment or otherwise.

We must encourage the participation of all in political life, as equals and as citizens, not as members of this or that particular community.

The foundation of this participation can be one thing and one thing only: the right to speak one's mind.

I remain, sir, your obedient servant.

Abraham Isaac

Attached by a rusting paper clip to the yellowing carbon copy of the original submission is a clipping from *The Straits Times*, head-lined 'Equal Not Separate'. The text is smaller than the typescript of the carbon copy. I need not bother to bring out my magnifying glass to read it, for the letter must surely have appeared complete and uncut.

The day that it appeared a number of colleagues made a point of congratulating me. Wasn't that the day I had my first serious discussion with Krishna? He was my fellow representative to the union, and he sought me out to announce his disagreement.

"This is very wishy-washy. It is not enough to be equally free to participate in politics. We are equally free to dine at the Raffles, but we neither of us can afford that pleasure. An agenda for social change, Abraham, an agenda for social change." His voice slowed for emphasis, as if he were addressing a union meeting. "Freedom is meaningless unless there are jobs, houses, education."

"Am I denying that? This letter only addresses one point — are we to be a nation of equals regardless of race and religion or are we to have separate communities, coming together only at the top, a coalition of different races?"

"Irrelevant question. Let us have a progressive platform first. Then we can choose between separate representation or equal participation depending on which is more popular, which will keep the right men in power to get on with what matters."

"Such as?"

"Industrial self-sufficiency. Better housing. This S.I.T. is a joke. Here we are, perhaps the richest spot in Asia, and some people live in slums. Government has to take charge: clear the slums, acquire the land, build cheap housing. But at the same time make sure that we control movement over the Causeway. People, I mean, not trade. Otherwise every time you improve conditions in the city all the kampong dwellers who don't even know how to use the *jamban* will come flooding in."

For a moment his face bobs in my memory, his teeth flashing white beneath a trim moustache and short curly hair. His skin was dark, but his eyes were bright and filled with mischief, so that no matter how serious he appeared to be when talking politics I always expected him at any moment to break into smiles and say he was only teasing. I respected his opinions, yet felt always on the verge of irritation, for the man assumed the air of someone a few steps ahead of his contemporaries. Damn the fellow for his presumption, for his belief that everything he might do was right, no matter how much his friends might get hurt in the process. Well, the man's luck ran out in the end.

Why does that thought bring me no satisfaction? Why am I unable to contemplate his memory with equanimity? I turn away from such questions, turn back to the folder.

Amongst the press clippings, letters to the press, a copy of a speech I once made to a union meeting (how many days of thought and worry went into that speech, attempting to find the right balance of fiery radicalism and administrative competence!), I espy, unfamiliar in this context, a corner of green letter paper. It has to be a letter from Rose, filed in the wrong place.

My dear Abraham,

I was so pleased and proud to receive the newspaper clipping that you sent me. I think that you expressed the point very well indeed, and that it was a point that demanded to be made. Charles read it and is in full agreement.

I was somewhat concerned to learn that Mercy has given up her work as a teacher, but am reassured that in your view it is best for her to concentrate, at this time, on her husband. I take it that you are hopeful of good news in that regard.

I, dear Abraham, have precisely that good news. I am expecting, praise the Lord. Charles' mother especially, but also his sister Jennifer, have been very kind, fussing over me. His sister drives, so sometimes she comes to take me out. One of my neighbours, a Welsh lady (she says we are fellow colonials, victims of the English — to members of which wicked race we are both married!), is also a great support.

At first, Abraham, I can admit now, I lacked confidence. Every-thing seemed so strange: the currency, the food, the weather. Every-thing was so grey, so cold, baths so occasional. The English are very austere, and, even though rationing has long since ended, an enjoy-

ment of food appears to be regarded as sinful. Really, apart from the buildings, all stone and brick, elegant and well-built, no matter how humble the occupants, one would think that Singapore were more prosperous than England!

But now I am beginning to relax, to find my feet, and of course now I have this wondrous spark of life growing within me, a daily reminder of the possibility of miracles.

Abraham, you are now secure in your job, your sister is married, surely it is your turn? I hope to hear good news from you soon.

Yours ever,

Rose

Eleven

I sit in my room, stiff and straight-backed on the chair, facing the window. The lights are off, but the fan revolves slowly overhead. The curtains are undrawn, the aluminium shutters open so that the corridor lights stripe the room into alternating bands of light and darkness.

How could she, how could she have done it to me?

It was late at night, the house shrouded in darkness except for the pool of light at my desk. I had been reading, yes, I can remember even now, John Stuart Mill's *Utilitarianism,* its cover dark and sombre, the title typeset in heavy and portentous lettering. I had been dreaming of a new nation, the possibility of rational men in power, disinterestedly taking those decisions that tended to the public good, seeing myself perhaps among them, Abraham Isaac, ushering in a new age of enlightenment, a new order, when I was roused by the shrill ring of the telephone. Striding quickly to it, anxious lest the noise awake my parents, I was ready to reprimand the caller for the lateness of the hour.

"Annai, is that you?"

"Mercy, it's very late. We're all in bed."

"I had to speak to you. It's David ..."

"What's the matter? Has he had an accident?"

"No, it's me ..."

"You've had an accident? What is it?"

"No …"

"Then why are you calling?"

"Annai, I can't stand it." Her voice rose to a wail. "He won't let me smoke and his mother … his mother …"

"It's not good for you to smoke."

"His mother, she keeps on and on and on about a baby."

"Why should she? She knows you're trying, aren't you?"

There was no reply except for Mercy's sobs. The woman was hysterical. If only she were present in front of me I could slap her face and snap her out of this nonsense.

"Mercy, pull yourself together. David is a good man, I know."

"What do you know?"

"Mercy, if you're going to talk like that … Look, you should go to sleep. Things will be different in the morning."

Silence.

"Mercy, what will David think of all this nonsense?" Still silence, a silence that provoked, set the words tumbling in a torrent. "Look here, Mercy, there's no point in working yourself up. Sleep first. Then in a day or two you and David should come over for dinner. You'd like that, right? I'll ask Amma to invite both of you …"

"He won't come …" The words seemed to speed like bullets across the telephone line. "He looks down on Appa, and on you."

The woman was hysterical. She was just trying to stir me to anger against David, but for what reason I could not fathom. "Where is he now?"

"Working, drinking, I don't know … he …"

"Mercy, you shouldn't talk like that … not about your husband. Go now and sleep."

"Annai, you're my brother, my elder brother, but you never look after me."

"Mercy, I don't know what you mean. David is there to look after you."

"It's no use. I can't ... Goodnight. Goodbye."

"Go and sleep now. Goodnight."

That at least is how I remember it. Whether it had taken place exactly like that, with Mercy's hysteria bubbling up only after her first few sentences, evaporating into rock-hard silence and then finally reviving with double its original vehemence, or whether she had simply been hysterical throughout, I cannot now be sure. How could I take her seriously, when her words were obviously the product of that girlish nonsense to which she was so prone?

I did return to my book, but how could I have been able to concentrate? My mind must have been distracted by concern for my sister. What was the matter with her? She had always been stubborn, yet I had come to believe that she was prepared to make the adjustments necessary for married life. I only hoped that she had not expressed her feelings in the old way, such as pouring hot tea on David's lap, or worse still on David's mother. I imagined that old lady, her thinning white hair tied up in a bun, her dry bony hands struggling to pull her sari away from her flesh at those parts where the scalding hot tea had soaked through the fabric. Intolerable! Imagine the scandal!

Eventually I must have settled back to my reading, to the science of managing means towards desired ends, the role of representative government in the achievement of this task at a national level, and the fundamental importance, nonetheless, of personal liberty, the first essential in the development of the individual as a progressive being.

At one point I tried to sleep, putting down the book, switching off the desk lamp and going to bed. But at that time I always found it hard to sleep. Mill's arguments (or whatever I had been reading that day) would race through my mind. Even lying motionless in bed, my eyes tightly shut, I would become dizzy. This no doubt must have prompted me to resume reading, even as the night outside grew darker.

A little after 3 a.m. a car swung into the driveway, its headlights sending shadows chasing through the house. My mind dulled by lack of sleep, I shambled towards the front door.

Looking through the grille that extended across the doorway, I watched David emerge from the driver's seat. The engine was still running and, as he crossed the beam of the headlights, he became, momentarily, a black shadow.

"Where is she?"

"Who?"

"Don't be funny. Who else would I be looking for?"

David had come up close to the front door, so that there was only a foot, and the metal grille, between us. His eyes were blood-shot, his mouth twisted. There was whisky on his breath. Just as Mercy had said, only for me to upbraid her.

"She's not here."

"Liar. How do you know who I'm talking about if she's not here? Where else would she be?"

"She's not here. Don't call me a liar."

"Open up." The man was bellowing.

"I will. If only to show you she's not here. But you must not wake my parents." I surprised myself by the firmness of my voice.

David looked away, then back at me.

"Of course I won't. I'll be very quiet."

"Switch off the motor first."

He did so, and the headlights too, while I unlocked the grille and pulled it open. My brother-in-law entered the front room, his head jerking around wildly, checking all the corners of the room. Then he looked at me and a cunning smile formed on his face.

"She's hiding with her parents, in her parents' room."

"No, David, stop …"

But it was too late. David had run down the short length of hallway and thrown open the door of our parents' room.

"Meeerrrcy!" It was a long drawn-out shout that began in sharp accusation, then wavered, ending in what sounded almost like a plea for forgiveness.

I reached the door only a stride behind him. Father had jerked upright, his face clearly visible in the light cast through the open door. Fear, then anger, passed over his features. Mother half-rose, then fell back into the darkness beside Father.

"What is it? What in God's name?"

David made no answer. He was crying, slowly sinking to his knees.

The rest of the night passed in a haze, a blue-grey fog of driving along dark and quiet streets, a haze punctuated by stops at the homes of Mercy's friends, of no help even if they could be stirred from sleep, and then dissolving into more driving that grew ever more aimless as the sky began to lighten and other cars appeared on the roads.

The police found her first. They had telephoned David's parents' house half an hour before we arrived there, the sky already tinged with pink but the air still cool. I was chilled from the wind upon my face. My throat was parched and I longed so much for a hot drink, Milo or even coffee, that all thoughts of Mercy had been driven from my head.

David's parents were in the front room. The mother was crying, her eyes red and swollen. His father was standing by the front door.

"Mercy has shamed us."

Anger rose from the pit of my stomach, swelling my chest.

"She has killed herself."

Suddenly I saw him, his face swollen with drink, fists etching bruises into her body. I wanted to scream, to shout, to batter David with my fists. Tear away his mask of learning, smash his pretence to the art of healing. *Murderer.* The word was on my tongue, yet I did not speak. Something held me back and I stepped outside, struggling to put my racing thoughts in order. The dog appeared, emerging from the shadows, its tongue lolling from its eagerly grinning mouth. "Wretched cur," I spat out, half-hoping that David, trembling on a chair within, would think the reference was to him.

Of course, I should have thrashed the bugger, then and there, when I still had the strength to do it. Look at me, sitting in this chair, the light from the corridor striping me like a convict from an old cartoon, my shoulders hunched, my arms leaning on the desk. I've left it too late, everything too late. That moment, as anger flamed first within my breast, I should have struck at least one blow of vengeance, for Mercy's sake. For Mercy, my dear, dear sister, for Mercy. Now it is too late, and I can never be forgiven for my inaction. "Mercy," I breathe, the palms of my hands pressed together, in an attitude of prayer.

The funeral took place on the following day. Thankfully the church was sufficiently enlightened to accept the funeral. "The manner of her passing is between her alone and the Lord," the priest had reassured us.

During the service the sky was overcast, the air swollen with the expectation of rain. The church was not filled. Many were not present who, not so very long before, had attended the wedding.

David of course was there, his face bloated with grief, his presence a provocation. His mother accompanied him, her face tense and strained but with no sign of tears. His father did not come.

Lily Chinappa approached me at the entrance to the church, a moment after the hearse doors had closed on the coffin. As if it were only yesterday I can remember how, as she extended her hand, her body seemed to back away, seemingly wary of contagion. Damn the lot of them.

Watching my parents share tears with my paternal uncle's family, I saw how the dishonour bound up in Mercy's choice of death caused to them the profoundest pain. Mercy, after all, had inherited their blood. Why did they submit so quietly, shouldering their burden of humiliation without a word of anger against him who was the true cause?

Few of the congregation followed the hearse to the cemetery, for, by the time the service was over, the skies had opened. The rain, taking on the colour of the clay soil, ran red between the graves. The grass was slippery and the footing uneven, so of the women who had accompanied the hearse, all of them clad in elegant saris and flimsy slippers, only Mother risked the indignity of falling by following the coffin to the grave. I left the carrying of the coffin to the professional undertakers, for Mother needed an arm to lean on and another to hold an umbrella, somewhat ineffectively, above our heads. I guided her gently to the head of the grave, which was protected from the rain by a tarpaulin, anchored at each corner and along the sides by bricks. The tarpaulin was then pulled away and the coffin lowered slowly into its resting place. The priest concluded the rites, throwing a clod of wet clay onto the coffin. Father followed suit, then I, pausing before letting the clay slip from my hand. I held my hand up to the rain, letting it wash off the red stain.

A few days after the funeral, forgetting my pride, neglectful even of my dignity, I wrote to Rose a letter spotted with my tears. It was a letter that I soon wished I had not dispatched, for I had addressed Rose with a frankness only possible with a wholly distant, perhaps invisible, confessor. Once I pictured her reading the letter, possibly in the kitchen, her hands washed for that purpose, interrupting the chopping of vegetables or the cleaning of fish, I regretted the candour of the epistle. How could she understand me at such a distance, not be critical of the stand I had taken? Such resolution might not be as Christ counselled, but surely when a man has behaved as David had done it could not readily be forgotten or forgiven.

I received her reply with a not inconsiderable trepidation, and let it lie upon my desk for a day or more unopened. At last I took my knife to it.

My dear Abraham,

When I read your letter I wept. I could not stop. I lay down in our bedroom, the curtains drawn against the afternoon sun, and thought of all the times we spent together. Mercy was a fine spirit, perhaps too spirited for this drab and dreary world. Do not blame David. Still less yourself, Abraham. Perhaps it was God's plan to remove her from a suffering she could not endure — I know what the priests say, what Mercy did was a sin, yes in the abstract perhaps, but only God truly knows why we do things, and I for one am sure she will not be condemned a sinner.

Abraham, you must not spend the rest of your life in mourning. Repentance and prayer are important, but they should not consume your life. Bitterness must be overcome. Look outwards, look to others. You have a lot to offer.

May God bless and keep you.

Yours ever,

Rose

How could she blame me for Mercy's death? Had I not always taken care of her? The audacity! Writing from thousands of miles away, having long since abandoned her own family in Singapore, she dared to apportion blame, grant dispensation and offer encouragement like some distant deity. It was my own fault; I had made this possible. I had raised her on a pedestal, so why should I be surprised that she believed herself raised in judgment above me?

Twelve

It's funny how even the worst memories pass, and one's mind, of its own accord, moves on to happier times. I put away the letter, switch off the reading lamp and settle back into bed.

Dismayed by Rose's letter and knowing no one who might share my grief and anger, I threw myself into work at school. Labour is perhaps the greatest virtue: I worked harder at lessons, striving to win rather than command the interest of the pupils. For a while I gave up the tracts that I had been studying and turned over my evenings to preparing for the next class. At first I was nervous about departing from time-honoured lesson formats. These were built around the assignment of poems to recite from memory, or else the prescription of Latin texts for which an authoritative translation had, as with the poetry, to be memorised. I was equally nervous about abandoning traditional forms of discipline: the throwing of chalk at any pupil who dared to talk to a neighbour during class or the use of a ruler on the palms of errant boys. I worried, how I worried, that forsaking the old ways might cause an immediate descent into anarchy, but believed that real learning took place in spite of, rather than because of, the old methods.

So, fortified by the conviction that these were new times that demanded new methods and bold action, I began to seek the boys' understanding of what they had been tasked to translate. I strove to win them over by my earnestness, by the effort that I put in, by my breadth of knowledge and, most of all, by my delight in the poetry or the texts. At times I had to feign this, but believed any dissimulation to be justified by the ends that I sought. I had to make the boys believe that they were engaged in something important, something that, if they too worked hard, they would learn to enjoy, and from which they would benefit.

The central puzzle was how to motivate a pupil who might speak Hokkien, Tamil or Malay at home. English was already a foreign language, and Latin twice foreign. The old answer, self-fulfilling so long as the Empire endured, that Shakespeare and Virgil were the necessary accoutrements of the civilised man, and civilised men obtained the best jobs, crumbled with each step towards Independence.

One day, during a free period, I discussed this problem with Krishna in the staff room.

"I can see your problem. For me it's different. Most of the boys have already made up their minds whether Maths is important. If they want to be doctors, yes. If lawyers, no. So I just tell them what they have to learn, and help those who want to learn. But if I were you I would tell the boys this. The future is uncertain. If things don't change, or don't change much, then English and Latin will be useful for all the old reasons. But if things do change, then Britain will be the enemy, and everyone knows that one must know one's enemy. So know his language, know his culture."

"I can't tell them that."

"But it's true. And it's the great advantage we have. It's easy to know them. But they'll never know us — they think understanding us is a waste of time, that their civilisation has all the answers. That's their mistake."

"Perhaps."

"But you should be careful, Abraham. You're becoming too popular with your students. Some of the other teachers are unhappy. I heard Lim complain yesterday that you were staying back to give extra lessons. He's probably scared that he'll end up having to work harder, but he's making noise about lack of discipline among your pupils, claiming they're badly behaved, that the only reason why ..."

"That's so unfair." I could not contain my dismay and agitation.

"I know it is. But since when was life fair? He said that the only reason why you had to give extra lessons was because you were behind in the syllabus, and that you're behind in the syllabus because you can't control your class."

I took Krishna's words seriously. I was not so naïve as to believe that ideals prove themselves. My pupils would have to do well in the School Certificate Examinations or else I would be blamed for neglecting educational standards. But I refused to return to traditional methods. Instead I redoubled my efforts to win the interest and respect of my pupils. I took special care with the slower learners and the ones who seemed uncomfortable with my informality. The reward for my patience was the increasingly dedicated atmosphere of the classroom. At first some of the pupils resisted the changes. Perhaps they were worried that they could not cope with the additional freedom given to them, and feared that the absence of forced learning, euphemistically and somewhat fondly called 'spoon-feeding', would be reflected in poorer grades in the examinations. Or perhaps they found it easier to deal with a teacher who acted as a teacher and did not confuse things by becoming a friend. They had been cautious, holding back in class, refusing to participate fully in discussions. But then, as it became clear to them that they received more attention than before, and therefore more rather than less guidance, they began to open up to me.

There were moments also of pure inspiration. Those three boys who attended both my English and Latin classes — what were their names? I can recall their faces: one a little pudgy, another gaunt with black-framed glasses and thick lenses like a Maoist intellectual, the third … no, even his face I've forgotten. The Maoist, not that he ever was one, became Perm Sec … his name will come to me at least. Those boys were something special; they began to use the literature they studied to interpret the world around them. *Hamlet,* which I was always in danger of reading as a personal reproach of my failure to avenge Mercy's death upon David, was to them a study of the process of decolonisation. The ordinary Singaporean was like Hamlet, his heritage despoiled by the interloping colonising Claudius. How then to act? Vengeance or forgiveness? *The Aeneid* came to stand for all the problems of an island-state and the quest for nationhood, suggesting how one small city could in the end become the focus of a great empire. What days those were, when even literature seemed to speak to the spirit of the age! How I looked forward to those classroom discussions, and how hard the struggle, in my enthusiasm for these grand exegeses, not to lose sight of the authors' original concerns.

This was also the time when I grew closer to Krishna. We were about the same age, in a staff room dominated by old and weary men. My suspicion that he was deeply involved in politics was confirmed when he introduced me to a new political party. Krishna proclaimed it to be the party of the future. It was not made up of tired and privileged liberals who in their hearts lamented the imminent passing of British rule, nor had it fallen prey to the naïvety of the Communists, who thought that, once they had exterminated their political enemies, there would be a brotherhood of man. These men were hard-headed practical types, who knew how to make things work. Sure, they were in politics for power, but who wasn't? They were Socialists, and so would direct their skills and talent, not simply to strengthening their own positions, but also to securing the common good.

I became a member of the Party, and took on greater responsibilities within the Teachers' Union. The Union had become an increasingly vocal and influential part of the Civil Service Union, and I became involved in the publication of a newsletter. This we produced as cheaply as possible. I would spend hours with the production team, cranking the handle of the cyclostyling machine, sorting the pages and stapling them together. Those hours together quickly generated strong feelings of solidarity. We worked in an office on the second storey of a shophouse in Tanjong Pagar. Beneath the office was a *kopi tiam* to which we would adjourn for *kopi* and *char siew pao*. Krishna would sometimes turn up, although he was less involved in the Union, and more involved in the Party. Then we would talk into the small hours. Our discussions grew longer and more heated as the first elections which would result in real, albeit limited, self-government approached.

I remember my disappointment when the Party announced that it would field only four candidates in the elections. This seemed a foolish move. The Party would be doomed to opposition, leaving an opportunity for another political party to take power and consolidate its grip prior even to full independence. But after a night of argument I accepted Krishna's position that the time was not right to take over the reins of government. Any government would be hamstrung by the continuing supervision of the British and in particular would be torn between the need to press for immediate independence and the need meanwhile to provide orderly and efficient administration. By staying out of government the Party would avoid this dilemma. It could call vehemently for full independence, spreading its influence among the rank-and-file while leading agitation against the government's sloth in achieving independence. At the same time, if the government failed to keep order it could be criticised for its inability to govern effectively. If, on the other hand, the government had to crack down on striking unions or rebellious students in order to maintain its grip, it could be reviled as a stooge and lackey of the British. I can't help but admire his perspicacity.

About that time I penned an article for the newsletter in which I analysed the political stances of the various parties and the personalities who were their candidates. The article was quiet and reflective in tone — I was after all addressing teachers and not a rabble — but it unmistakeably reached the firm conclusion that the Party was the only one which had both the vision and the ability to guide Singapore's future. When the newsletter containing the article was distributed, the principal summoned me. I entered his office righteous, mind made up that I should appear indignant even at the fact that such an interview could be regarded as necessary. But I doubt that that firm sense of righteousness could have entirely stopped my stomach's nervous churning.

The principal was at his desk writing when, after knocking, I entered. He was an Englishman, a tall man, but with his head turned down towards his notepad, I could see how red and blotched was the scalp of his balding crown. He sought in vain to conceal this condition by combing strands of wispy blond hair across it.

After a few moments the principal looked up and gestured towards the stiff-backed chairs placed in front of his desk. I sat down. A few moments later the principal put down his pen and looked up.

"I read your article. Fine piece of writing. Now, I have no objections to it or to your continued involvement in the Union or in politics or whatever. I've also heard good things about your teaching. A number of parents have said that their sons have become much more interested in English and Latin, and much more hardworking, because of your teaching. Keep it up. I have just one thing to say."

I curled my lip, to express contempt for the censure that must follow.

"Please exercise your discretion carefully. Remember, the pupils' success in exams comes first. Their political awareness second. That's all."

I stood up and left, disappointed that there had been no confrontation, no opportunity to prove commitment to the independence movement and disdain for the colonial government. When Krishna questioned me afterwards I could not resist hinting at a severe rebuke by the principal, nor could I withhold a shrug of my shoulders to suggest defiance in the face of all threats.

A youthful boast. It had shaded into a falsehood by which I had sought to mark myself out from the general mass of mediocrity. What vanity, and yet surely it cannot be said that my life has been wholly ordinary. Even if I did not act to punish David as I ought to have done, have I not, in the end, nonetheless distinguished myself by my courage, or at least by some quality of steadfastness of which I can be proud?

Thirteen

*S*oon after the general elections, in which all but one of the Party's candidates had been successful (thus forming a small, cohesive and virulent grouping in the legislative assembly), Father took me aside and suggested that it was about time that a bride was found for me.

"I want to choose my own wife. Someone who loves me."

"You have no time to look. Amma and I, we have the knowledge, and the time. Let us do the looking. Of course we give you the final say."

After a moment's hesitation, I accepted. It sounded sensible enough and what harm, after all, could it do? Within a fortnight mother had four photographs with accompanying descriptions of family background, character and interests for me to study. I went through them, and found only one girl who might be suitable, because she was working and a little older than the others, while still a good four years younger than I was. I wanted someone with a mind of her own, who would choose me of her own free will. I pledged to nurture her independence, and never repeat even one of David's sins. Her name was Rani, Rani Supramaniam. She had (or so it appeared from the photograph) a strong face made up of bold features: large sparkling eyes, full firm lips and high pronounced cheekbones. She worked as a primary-school teacher.

My parents met with hers and terms were settled contingent only upon her and my decision. The first meeting would be at her house the following Saturday afternoon.

I was anxious to make the right impression. Mother had carefully ironed my best white shirt, and I wore that over a singlet which would, I hoped, absorb any sweat my nervousness might produce. I wore a tie, in fact, as I recall, my school tie, and a pair of dark trousers that had been recently tailored. Mother had polished my black leather shoes, and, though they had seen considerable wear, I trusted them to suggest nothing other than a judicious mix of respectability and frugality.

The lady who had made the introduction arrived to escort us to the Supramaniams'. She was a stout elderly widow who looked me over with such a stern appraising air that I half-expected her to start touching and poking as if I were a fruit whose quality and freshness were in doubt. After that inspection she ignored me and started talking to Mother about the family and social connections of the Supramaniams. Father and I did not talk during the drive. The car was filled with the chatter of the women. But, when we had parked opposite the Supramaniams' semi-detached house, Father reached across and squeezed my arm in a gesture of masculine complicity that simultaneously embarrassed and heartened me.

Mother and the matchmaker led the way into the compound. The parents (I guessed) together with two men, perhaps a little younger than I was (her brothers?), stood on the porch, waiting to greet us. Introductions followed, and I received what I took to be an encouraging smile from her mother. I congratulated her on the appearance of the house, although I really thought it rather bare and even a little dusty, and she deflected my praise towards her daughter who, she said, was very tidy and hardworking.

No sooner had I settled into an armchair than Rani emerged from the back of the house, accompanied by the tinkling of her bangles and of an anklet hung with tiny chimes. Her sari was a pleasant mix of greens, a stylised pattern of leaves and vines. As I stood up to greet her I caught a waft of her fragrance, sandalwood, yes, but mingled with another scent that seemed to tickle me between the eyes. She looked briefly up at me before demurely lowering her lashes (what long curly lashes!) and gazing at the floor. I was enchanted.

And struggled to concentrate in order to answer her father's questions about work, managing only generalities about the school, the mix of pupils, the hours and my prospects for promotion. Then came a different kind of question, more insistent that a precise answer be given.

"We hear that you are involving yourself in union politics. Are you sure this is wise?"

"Mr Supramaniam, my involvement is slight. I write for the Union newsletter, and of course sometimes we have to comment on the political scene."

"You say it is slight now, but how about the future? Abraham, I ask because we are not the majority here. Should we really be in politics at all?"

"Perhaps we have to make up our minds where we belong. Wherever we belong we must get involved."

"And these Chinese people are different from us. Politics can never be a game to them. Played for fun. With rules. For them politics is deadly serious. And about one thing only. Power. And making money."

"I think you are speaking of China. Malaya is different. We have had the British here for too long. We have heard so much about fair play. Now we will put it into practice."

"I don't want to press you, Abraham. But I hear also you have links to this radical party, some say it is almost a Communist party. Is that safe?"

"I think those people are wrong. It is the party of the future. If you are concerned about my safety I tell you it is safer to be with them than against them."

Mr Supramaniam turned his gaze to Father. The interrogation appeared at an end.

"Politics, politics. In my time we never had to worry about such things. The British took care of everything. Am I speaking correctly, Isaac?"

Father shook his head from side to side in agreement. At that moment Rani came back into the room with a tray of cups filled with tea. She set the tray down on a side table. Bending a little awkwardly over the tray, she could almost have been Mercy. At once I stood up to help. Mrs Supramaniam waved me away, urging me to resume my seat, but I remained standing, awkwardly, until Rani had set down my cup of tea on the table next to my armchair. As she did so she flashed a smile up at me, revealing her teeth. I noticed for the first time that they stuck out a little in front. As she turned to leave the room a quiver of desire ran through me.

"Speaking frankly, young man, I understand you want to get to know my daughter first, am I right?"

Before he could answer, the matchmaker had rattled off in Tamil, almost too fast for me to catch, "Young people, modern world", causing both the mothers to laugh.

"Yes sir."

"Very well. My son, George," he looked across the room at one of the two men, "yes, you boy, will accompany the two of you. I suggest tomorrow afternoon, four o'clock, cakes and tea at Polar Cafe. Is that agreeable?"

"Yes sir."

The last thing I wanted was to be shadowed by Rani's brother. Why was traditional Tamil culture based on the assumption that no young man (other than a brother) could be trusted with the virtue of a young lady? But I had no choice: my life would inevitably be made up of such little compromises between modern values and traditional expectations. But at least I could counteract the brother's presence by enlisting Krishna as a second chaperon. He immediately agreed, perhaps more from curiosity than helpfulness, so the next day the two of us were standing outside the Polar Cafe, waiting for Rani and her brother, by a quarter to four.

"I hope she turns up. She may have cold feet. You must be rather a formidable prospect."

"She'll be here. Remember, keep the brother busy. I want her to react to me naturally — not always worrying about the report her brother will make to her parents."

"Don't worry. When have I ever let you down? I'll keep James occupied."

"George, Krishna. His name is George."

"Hey, don't be so nervous. I'm only joking. I know his name is Charles."

"Shut up." How had Krishna chanced upon a name that inevitably shook my equanimity? I struggled to master myself and appear unruffled. "Here they come."

Rani, to my surprise, was wearing a dress instead of a sari. She was wearing sunglasses. Their black frame curved upwards at the corners like cat's eyes.

"Jesus Christ," Krishna whispered from the corner of his mouth. "You lucky bugger."

We settled at a corner table. Krishna ordered curry puffs and ginger beer, and did his job well, although his eyes kept straying from George to Rani. I talked to her about teaching, telling a funny story about a colleague, asked questions about her school, and then rattled on about books that, after enquiry, I had discovered we had both read. My cheeks grew hot in my excitement, and, finally, touching her hand briefly as I gazed into her face, my confidence growing, I turned to my ambitions — to be a good teacher, respected by my pupils, not feared; to be a good citizen of our new nation; to contribute to the community; and (here we both looked down) to be a good husband and father to my family, God willing.

I fell silent. Krishna, a slight smile on his face, suggested it was time to leave. We did so, and stood on the pavement outside until a taxi had been hailed for George and Rani. Before she stepped gracefully into the taxi, she turned to me.

"You are a good, kind man. Next week at the same time and place?"

"Yes, God yes." She seemed to frown a little. Careless tongue to make vain mention of His name! But her face cleared immediately, and she smiled and waved as the taxi pulled away from the curb.

Krishna teased mercilessly, but I hardly noticed. My mind was adrift then as it is now in thoughts of Rani: that moment when she bit into a curry puff, her rosy lips parted, her white teeth pressing forward, or when my hand brushed hers, setting us both trembling. O wicked cruel courtship that tantalised me so!

So my life settled into a pattern of weekdays when I would burn for her, she who held sway over my mind even as I taught a class or tried distractedly to compose an article for the Union newsletter, and Sunday afternoons when my heart would dance in her presence, while Krishna kept George busy with curry puffs and ginger beer. Sometimes we would go for a walk, Krishna pushing George on ahead while Rani and I dawdled behind. We would look in at shop windows: tailor's shops, dress shops, jeweller's shops, bakeries and photographer's studios. In our wanderings we slowly built up a consensus of taste: clothes, food, books, ideas — a whole world of opinions that we gradually matched and weaved together. Hesitant at first, we grew more confident, as the weeks went past, in our shared judgment, until I was certain that, if I asked her whether she loved me, she would say yes.

Two days before the Sunday on which I had resolved to seek Rani's commitment to me, a letter arrived from Rose. This confirmed me in my belief that the time was right to settle on marriage with Rani, because, for the first time, I felt no regret, no longing for Rose, no matter that she penned to me the homeliest of details, stories of her now three-year-old son, or of the new life that stirred once again within her. There was no hatred now for Charles, who had taken Rose away. I could see her in perspective: a childhood fancy, no more. I had put her on a pedestal, and she had proved to be merely human. Those thoughts of Rose, her heaving bosom, her soaring voice, her face framed by the morning sun, were pushed aside, no, totally overwhelmed, by Rani, her eyes that widened as I told of my dreams, her mouth, seemingly fixed in a perpetual and utterly endearing pout, her soft fragrant body, each tiny detail that made up the magnificent whole.

So I proposed. And Rani said, "How slow you are! Perhaps I watched you too much, like water that one hopes to boil on the stove."

When we had caught up with George and Krishna, and George and Rani had been despatched for home, I told Krishna the news.

"Certainly it is good news, for I am sick and tired of those curry puffs. As for young George, not only is he a boring ass, but his face has grown very much to resemble a curry puff: pasty, oily and puffy."

"But no fiery filling inside!"

108

"No, I think you and Rani monopolised the hot stuff. But really I shall miss not seeing Rani on a Sunday afternoon. And my hopes that you two might not hit it off so that I might have a chance are totally blown." Krishna laughed, as if to reassure me that he was only joking.

"But of course you shall see us both, and often I hope. To start with, you must be my best man."

"Delighted, Mr Isaac, delighted!"

Fourteen

My dearest Abraham,

I write with good news. I shall be visiting Singapore again, the land of my birth. I shall also be travelling to Colombo, but I am not sure yet whether it will be safe to travel to Jaffna, our poor, war-torn, ancestral homeland. I grieve for Jaffna, and pray for our salvation every night.

I expect to be coming around Christmas. I will probably go to Colombo first, then come out to Singapore. I shall be there perhaps three weeks or so before Charles and the boys join me. Charles' work keeps him very busy, not just at the High Court but also out on circuit. He had thought becoming a judge would lessen his workload, but that has not really proved to be the case. The result in any event is that he can only spare a couple of weeks, but he is quite excited nonetheless, although he has expressed dismay at some of the changes in Singapore's legal system over the years.

Needless to say, I am very excited. Singapore was always a busy, bustling place, but I hear that nowadays it is even more so. And it is more than thirty years since my last visit. I wonder if there will be anything I can recognise. I am told that a new subway system *has just been installed, that it is desperately modern, and everyone is terrifically proud of it.*

I should not ramble on so. I thought I should just give you some advance warning. I will of course be staying with Lily.

I will write again once I know the date of my arrival.

May God bless and protect you.

Yours ever,

Rose

As I replace the letter in its envelope, anxiety mingles with pleasure. She must not find a tired, lonely old man. At least in letters one can dissemble a little, rationalise one's life, pretend to an equanimity one does not possess. But I too have contributed, even if I cannot compete with Charles' achievements. But for him how much easier things have been. It was simply a matter of dedicating one's life to serving a system whose justice (if one excepts the Communists) is universally acknowledged and admired. Singapore is different. A new system had to be built. Some had different visions of the most just system, while others scrambled merely for power and influence. How could I have been expected to keep my balance in the shifting sands?

Everything was so different when she last visited. I it was who had chosen rightly; soon to be citizen of a proud young nation. She had married into an Empire that was everywhere in retreat. What glory the future held in store, for Singapore and for me. For her there could surely only be regrets, the loss of home and family, the warmth of St John's. She had given up so much for Charles ... to my chagrin, of course, but by the time of her visit I had long since overcome my jealousy.

It was soon after my marriage that she visited, a year or so before the elections that would sweep the Party into power. Her elder son, then about five, accompanied her, while her younger boy was left to the care of Charles' parents.

I was flushed with the happiness of wedlock. Against the wishes of my parents I had refused, mindful of my sister, to bring my bride home to my parents' household. Instead we set up together, in a flat off Haig Road. This was hardly altogether unorthodox, for Katong, at least a little inland (not the coast with its elegant mansions and rich men's parties that swayed to the sensual rhythms of the sea), had become the preferred area for the Jaffna Tamil community. Yet Mother nonetheless disapproved of our arrangements. She brought food every few days, lest her only son be starved by an incompetent daughter-in-law, but at least her influence was at one remove. We were free to adjust to one another as husband and wife, as equals, unconcerned about any other roles we might have to play, not son, not daughter-in-law. I left it to her to organise the kitchen as she pleased, but took upon myself a great deal more responsibility for the rest of the housework than Father ever had. This could only be fair, since after all both of us were working.

Father questioned me on the necessity of making my wife work, seeming to suggest that it could only be a lack of masculine vigour on my part that could bring about such an unsatisfactory state of affairs. But I was firm in my response, explaining that it was not so much a question of necessity as independence, that it was better for Rani to have a job for her own self-respect, and this he finally appeared to accept. Mother was even less sympathetic: "Since when was it not enough for a woman to look after her husband and her children? That by itself is a full-time job." I did not argue, suggesting only that things might change when children came along. That qualified assurance was no doubt insufficient to satisfy her, but at least it kept her quiet. I did not mention that we had no plans to have children immediately.

Our first night was almost a disaster. Better schooled in most things than in the task I was then called upon to perform, I fumbled in the dark, moving clumsily from side to side. After a while, just as I was about to stop and claim that I had accomplished all that was necessary, she broke the silence that, like the darkness, had concealed our discomfiture.

"I don't think this can be the right way."

I froze. For a moment grievance built up within me. Who was she to tell me I was not doing it right? What sort of idiot was I that I did not know what to do? And, worst of all, how did she know anyway?

In that moment I could have leaped from the bed, shouting abuse at her. But something in her voice, perhaps just its gentleness, made me pause. It was true. I was not doing it right. And why shouldn't she know? Her mother would have spoken to her, perhaps even some of her married friends. Men were full of boasts, not information. Why shouldn't she know? I relaxed in her arms. "Give me a hand," I whispered, and she did.

But, although I became at least technically competent, I remained embarrassed, wary of my own desire, the strength of which frightened me at times. I would rush into an embrace, darkness my cloak, seeking release as soon as possible.

Nonetheless, at the time of Rose's visit, I had felt blissfully secure in my marriage. Rose came to our flat for tea, and I showed her around, proud of our possessions: the new Ferguson radio on the sideboard, the clock hanging on the wall that chimed the hours, the bright new carpet in the living room.

Rose made herself comfortable at one end of the sofa. Her son sat on the floor with an alphabet book. He was, she said, learning to read and write. Occasionally he would get bored and start running round the room with his arms outspread, making sounds like an aeroplane. At those times Rose would scold him, and he would settle back to the book. His name was Harold, but he answered only to Harry, and would pout if called by his full name. He was a handsome child: thick black hair and a golden complexion — a fortuitous combination of Charles' pasty pink and Rose's glossy brown.

We chatted, talking of old times, of friends and relatives and what had become of them. After Rani had brought out the tea and some cakes that she had made, she sat on the arm of my chair. Her possessive gesture irritated me. Surely she must realise that Rose was no threat to her. I did not want to give Rose the impression that, since my wife believed such gestures necessary, I must still lust after her. Yet I was also irritated that Rani was interposing herself between us. I had an old friendship with Rose, and did not want it mediated through Rani any more than through Charles.

Whatever the exact grounds of my irritation, when Rani went back to the kitchen to make more tea, I placed my arms firmly on those of the chair. The signal was not lost on Rani when she returned, and she sat down promptly on the other armchair.

But Rose too had seen the signal. What she had understood by it I could not tell, but when Rose had left, Rani ran to our bedroom in tears.

I followed her in. She was lying face down on our bed.

"What is it?"

She did not answer. I walked over to the bed and sat down beside her. I placed a hand on her shoulder. She shrugged it off, half-rising in order to do so.

"What's wrong? Please talk to me."

"How could you?"

"What do you mean?" I feigned innocence, although I knew very well what she meant.

"You still love her."

"Rani, don't say such things. I never loved her."

"You're lying."

"It's true. She was my childhood …" I searched for the right word. "… infatuation. That's what I told you, and it's the truth. I never loved her. I certainly don't love her now. I love you."

Rani quietened. "Then why did you stop me from sitting there, sitting on the arm?"

"Rani, please, it was just a little awkward, nothing more."

I bent down and kissed the back of her neck. Then I turned her around and held her.

"I'm sorry," she said. "Sorry to be so silly. It's just … I can't bear to think that part of you belongs to someone else."

"Hush, my little kitten."

The elections took place a few months after Rose's departure. The Party was swept into office. I was elated: now at last a vigorous hand could be set to the task of Singapore's development as an independent nation. While the city had always been prosperous, genuine political self-direction could alleviate problems, such as housing and sanitation, that had been glossed over by our imperial masters. Krishna, who had resigned from his job as a teacher in order to enter politics full-time and stand for elections, came into school to bask in the congratulations of his former colleagues.

"Bloody good show."

"Spectacular, though I say so myself. But the war's not over. We need good men like you in the unions. There's a lot of work to be done. Also, now you're married and settled down, how about doing more? Come and work in my constituency. Maybe you could be a candidate next time."

Krishna's interest pleased me. Yes, why not go into politics? That night, lying in bed, I spoke to Rani about it.

"Abraham dear, you must do as you think best. But Krishna is hard, practical. He can get things done. You are soft, a dreamer. I don't know if politics will be good for you."

"*Acha,* hard, soft … and which do you prefer?"

Rani looked serious, then stroked my cheek. "Soft here, I think …" She ducked her hand to my groin. "Maybe hard here." Her eyes were shining as I grabbed her, kissed her and in a rush, always in a rush, took her.

Before I could begin any practical steps towards deepening my political involvement, the new leadership, within a year of the elections, began to take steps to bring the Civil Service firmly under its control. I admit that at first I agreed with their actions. It was important for the Civil Service to respond to the political leadership, and so, indirectly, to serve the people. But when the head of the Civil Service Union objected to changes in terms and conditions of service which the new leadership sought unilaterally to impose, and the new leadership took aim at him and began to plot his removal, I became concerned.

I telephoned Krishna.

"This can't be right. You can't ride roughshod like that."

"It's not just a question of who's right and wrong in this particular instance. More important things are at stake. We have to show who's boss. Only if we're feared can we do what has to be done."

"I don't accept that."

116

"You will. Just keep your mouth shut."

Krishna's advice seemed sensible, but the wrongness of the new leadership's actions ached in my marrow. How could they act so ruthlessly against one man who was only standing up for what he believed to be right? How could they destroy one man's life just to frighten others? This was not what I had hoped for when I had supported a vigorous new government to tackle the nation's problems.

So I wrote a blistering defence of the Civil Service Union leader, which I had printed in the Teachers' Union newsletter. I wrote a letter to *The Straits Times* but it was not published, the newspaper's editorial stance having shifted dramatically following the victory of the Party.

The day after the newsletter was distributed, I was congratulated on the article by several colleagues. Just what they had believed. It was about time somebody said it. One couldn't stand by and let this kind of repression take grip of society. I felt like a hero, having done what was right and having caught the public mood at the same time. Others would see my actions and cease to be afraid. The new government would back down, its leaders examining their conscience and choosing the right path.

A few days later I was called into the principal's office. The principal was a local man now: a tall, lanky Chinese man with a thin wispy moustache. He was young, intelligent, ambitious. I expected at worst a cautionary word, at best an expression of support. Instead his tone was querulous.

"What do you think you are doing? This is not Chung Cheng. You can't organise protests, boycotts, whatever you please." The principal was bobbing his head, more nervously than challengingly.

"Sir, I haven't organised any boycott, any protest. I'm entitled to voice my opinions. I don't see what business this is of yours."

"Not my business? The bloody Ministry on my back and you say it's not my business? Come on Abraham. Retract your statements. Write a letter of apology to me, so I can pass it on to the Ministry. Or else … it's out of my hands."

Good sense suggested contrition. "I can't apologise. I spoke only what I believe to be the truth." I pulled back my shoulders and pushed out my chest, attempting to fix the principal's peripatetic head with a firm gaze.

"Look. I don't want to argue. You choose. I'll give you until four. Four o'clock." The principal's head stopped its wanderings momentarily as he looked up. "You don't come back, you don't apologise, you're fired."

"For what?"

"Conduct unbecoming to a teacher. Disruptive influence. We will see what the committee says."

"I'll fight. Goodbye."

I walked out of the principal's office, slamming the door shut, and strode to the staff room, angry and unbowed. I sat down and crossed my legs, then stood up again. I stood in silence, glowering at the floor, for what must have been some minutes. Then a colleague, one of those who had congratulated me on the article, came over.

"Tough luck. You did a brave thing." He did not look at me as he spoke, and began to turn away the moment he had finished.

"And that's it? Isn't anyone going to come out in support?"

"Don't ask too much. I have a wife and kids." He began in embarrassment but ended in defiance, as if the question was in itself an affront.

I looked around the staff room. None of the teachers met my eye. I turned to leave.

"Hey," said the man with whom I had just been speaking. "There's still time to back down. It's not worth it."

My pace did not slow. I had a class to teach. I walked down the corridor and up the stairs to the classroom where the lesson was to be held. My footsteps echoing off the concrete floor. The whole school hushed by the drama that was unfolding. Why was the classroom so quiet, I wondered, until, as I swung the door open, the answer revealed itself. Another teacher had arrived before me. It was Chong, a few years my senior and one of the few persons other than Tamils to worship at our church. Standing at the front of the classroom, writing on the blackboard, he looked round as the door opened. His expression of reproach softened into a sheepish smile as he realised that this was not a tardy pupil. The speed with which the principal had acted only deepened my rage.

"Get out. This is my class."

"Don't be like that, Abraham. I'm under orders from the principal. I think it is you who should leave. Don't make a bad thing worse."

I looked round at the anxious, worried faces of the schoolboys. I had no right to involve them in my quarrel.

"All right. I'm going. But you remember that I wanted to teach my class."

What else could I do but leave school? I took the bus home, startling Rani when I walked through the front door, at least two hours before she had expected me home. I explained what had happened, and was gratified that she took it so calmly. She did not ask me to apologise to the Ministry. She did not turn hysterical. Calmly, quietly, she asked me to ring Krishna. "He will help. He is a good man. He can stop this madness."

The telephone was engaged at first, but eventually I got through. It was not a good line, but through the crackles Krishna's message was loud and clear. An omelette could not be made without breaking eggs, and I was best advised not to be a bloody egg.

"You're washing your hands."

"I'm not washing anything. I'm giving you good advice."

"You're washing your hands."

"I'm not. Just think about it for a while." The dull tone of the disconnected receiver buzzed in my ear.

I look down at the envelope. In the fever of my remembrance I have crumpled it into a tiny ball. I place it on the desk and move my fist along it, a vain attempt to smoothen out the creases. The clock shows that it is already past the time that I should have started out for the Yeos' house. Memories seem to be overwhelming me, they seize me and will not let go. I must stop them. Choke them off. What is done is done. But the future, that is still in my hands. Richard takes the 'O' Level next week, and I have to make sure that he is fully prepared. A clever boy, that Richard, but you never know. A teacher can never sit back. He has to keep pushing.

Fifteen

*T*oday is the last revision session before Richard takes his 'O' Level. Anxious to avoid mawkishness, to maintain a professional demeanour, I begin briskly enough with two 'unseen' passages. Then a handful of sentences which involve particularly complex grammatical forms. Finally, some of the more difficult passages in the set texts. Yet inevitably, as the session draws to a close, I am tempted into a summing up.

"Good. Very good. Do you have any questions?"

"No, most things are pretty clear."

"That's how it should be. You're a good student. But don't forget, part of being a good student, part of being smart, is asking questions when you don't know something. That's how you learn."

"I know that. But sometimes I don't know when I don't know something."

"That's why I'm still running through 'unseens' and so forth."

"May I ask you, do you have any other students?"

Why does the boy ask that? For a moment it seems as if there is more than idle curiosity in such a question, perhaps even concern. "Latin is not a popular subject any more. People no longer respect learning for the sake of learning."

"Do you teach any other subjects?"

"English. But who speaks English well these days?"

Thus I fall into bitterness, self-deprecation that cries out for the response that sure enough follows. "You're a very good teacher. I've … learned a lot from you."

"I was a good teacher … once. Nowadays I just offer a little help here and there. A remedial tutor paid to raise some child's grades. I lost my vocation a long time ago."

"But you've taught me. You've taught me Latin from scratch."

"That I have. And I've enjoyed doing it. You've made me feel like a teacher again."

Silence, broken only by the whirring of the ceiling fan. I cannot speak, nor meet the boy's gaze. I try, yes I do, to bring things to a close, to avoid further embarrassment. "I should be going. Just run through the texts over the next few days by yourself, and you'll be fine. I don't suppose I'll see you before you leave for England."

"No, probably not. You said you've never been there, right?"

"No. I haven't. I have a friend who went to England. Married an Englishman. A judge now, you know." Richard stands up. I look at him and for some reason continue speaking, as if seeking to impress him.

"You know something. You know what that Englishman once said?" Richard shrugs his shoulders, shakes his head, but looks interested in the answer.

"He said he thought at first that I had been educated at Oxford."

The boy smiles, almost in amusement.

"But I wasn't, you know. I never was an Englishman. Never wanted to be. I wanted only to be a Singaporean."

"But you are."

"I'm just an old man." Confusion and pain cloud the boy's features. I cannot leave on that note, and so continue in a lighter tone of voice. "No, don't mind me. You, you're full of promise. You can do great things. But you have to be strong. It's not good enough just to do the right thing. You have to be strong enough to make what you do count. Maybe you can do that. But only if you will yourself to be strong enough. You can't depend on anyone else to help, not even someone you love, least of all someone you love."

"That can't be right. What's the point of love then?"

What am I thinking of, talking in such a fashion? I can only confuse the boy, and what really do I mean? I think of the boy's mother, of the illness she is struggling with, think of how much she must mean to him. He is quiet and sensitive, a mother's boy, weak, ultimately weak.

"Tell me what you mean." He has resumed his seat. I must finish.

"Some things can only be learned, not taught. These things can't be put into words. Loving someone is good, a wonderful thing, but it makes you weaker, more vulnerable. You love your mother so the pain she suffers becomes your pain."

"So I shouldn't love …" Despair fills his voice. I struggle to dispel it.

"No, no. Once more, no. That's why I say these things cannot be taught. You should love, you will love, you won't be able to stop yourself and you shouldn't try. Just will yourself to be strong enough to survive your love. I see from your eyes that you still don't understand. You mistrust my words. You think I am too old."

"No."

"Yes, you do. Perhaps I am." So finally, perhaps only to change the subject, I come to a point of which I have become almost convinced in recent days. "Listen. You know my name?"

"I'm sorry?"

"My name?"

"Mr Isaac. So?"

"My first name is Abraham. Do you know the story of Abraham and Isaac?"

"Yes. Sure I do. God tested Abraham's obedience — asked him to sacrifice his only son, Isaac. Abraham obeyed. He went up to the mountain with Isaac, tied him to the altar. At the last moment, when Abraham was about to … you know … God stopped him. He provided a ram for Abraham to slaughter instead."

"That's right. But have you ever thought of Isaac? At some point he must have realised what his father planned. Did he have such faith in God that He would intervene? How could he? He did not even know that God had spoken to his father. No, Isaac was ready to die. Why? Because he loved his father. He lay passively on the altar table, waiting for the knife. Love, boy, it leads you to sacrifice."

"Even Abraham, he was caught between two loves."

"Exactly. Sacrifice his son for the love of God. Or lose his soul for the love of his son. He was doubly vulnerable. And even though Isaac's life was spared by God, had not Abraham already betrayed his son?"

The boy is silent. For a while I am flushed with the force of my words, and take his silence to be concurrence with my views. For a moment or two I am sure that I have expressed a great insight into the struggles of my own life and offered in some profound way guidance for the boy's. Then I wonder what else can the boy say? His silence is probably no more than the product of bewilderment. In the end I have indulged in just that sentimentality, that absurd baring of the soul, that I steeled myself to eschew. Another old man passing on the burden of his years to a surrogate son. Why have I never been able to do a job simply, to see clearly what is required and what the limits are? Emotion has always blinded me. A misplaced imagining of significance in the trivial tasks and duties that constitute my life. I have grown silent, I must be puzzling and worrying the boy. I force myself to my feet.

"You just work hard. Do your best. Let me know how the exam goes. Send me the result."

And so I depart, leaving behind me the last of my pupils.

Sixteen

I was suspended from school pending the investigation of the charges. This was the responsibility of a committee appointed by the Board of Governors, on the recommendation of the principal. St George's, as its name suggests, is by origin a mission school, so the Ministry's control over the school's teaching staff and policies was indirect. The lack of direct control offered hope that, once the initial agitation had died down, I could convince the committee that I was no troublemaker. They would see that I was in fact a respected and responsible teacher, who had at no time stepped beyond the boundaries of proper and acceptable behaviour. In the Government schools teachers were not permitted to join political parties, but that was not the case in the mission and other quasi-independent schools. Indeed there were Members of Parliament for the Party who taught in such schools. Moreover, I was a member of the very Party that was now in government, not an opposition party. In that context, writing the article could be regarded as at most political commentary, and not political action. Teachers could not be expected to operate in a political vacuum.

I had a lot of time to consider my defence. Waking before Rani left for her school, I would make her tea and some toast. Then I would read *The Straits Times* for an hour, although this exercise became gradually more and more depressing as the coverage grew more uniform in its slant. The Party was starting a purge within its own ranks now, and a campaign was beginning in the newspaper against a particular Minister, a fiery speaker and a man with definite leadership ambitions. The man was being portrayed as incompetent, if not corrupt. That might well be true, but the problem was that it was increasingly impossible to tell, for only one position was ever properly reported. Other viewpoints were ignored or distorted.

I would sit and brood, sometimes in one armchair, sometimes the other. Or go back to bed, the curtains drawn shut, the ceiling fan whirring overhead. Towards mid-morning I would rouse myself and go to the market. I wondered at first why I lowered my voice and looked away as I spoke to the vendors at the Katong wet market, the sellers of fish, goat, chicken, vegetables or fruit. As the days passed, I understood that it was shame, shame that I, an ablebodied man, had nothing better to do than jostle with housewives, enduring the salt and vinegar smell of ocean and the sour, sweaty stink of the chickens pressed together in their wire coops, piled one on top of the other, in search of the freshest prawns, the ripest mango. At first I felt and seemed so out of place that I was almost invisible, ignored by the vendors and pushed past by the women, who called out their orders in a staccato lingo that I understood but was loath to master, for to make that effort was to accept that little distinguished me from its speakers.

Then, with my bags filled with produce for the evening meal, I would go to a nearby coffeeshop, order a *char kway teow* or a *nasi biryani,* and a glass of thick, sweetened, black local coffee. What was it that colleague had said, ex-colleague, in disparagement of this brew? The man had just arrived from England to teach for three years, and there he was laying down the law about the … yes that was it, the 'cloying creaminess' of local coffee. In vain had I explained that Singaporeans actually drink this mix of coffee beans,

126

chicory and margarine by choice and that its taste is richer than the thin and sometimes sour flavour of pure coffee. "Unlike you English," I had said, "we do not value austerity for its own sake. We are gluttons, not ascetics, by nature."

"Then you lot are even madder than I thought. Although David Hume teaches us desire precedes reason, that reason only tells us how best to fulfil our desires and not what desires to have, I am inclined to believe that liking this shit-coloured water is an irrational desire. It is not coffee: it is a debasement of that noble brew."

Pompous ass, I had thought, but kept my temper in check, instead venturing the remark that the way the English boiled cabbage was at least as irrational, and was amused that the man had not been able to understand what was wrong with that English way.

Now however I felt no burst of national pride as I drank. Rather I felt the coffee work its way through my system like a slow-acting poison, deadening my senses, not, as coffee ought to, pepping up my thoughts. Was this not the drink of old men, sitting around the marble-topped tables of innumerable coffeeshops across Singapore, talking of the good old days of hardship and sacrifice, setting up Chinese chess pieces on coffee-stained boards, stroking their whiskers and picking at hardening patches of skin on their aging dried-up bodies? Was I already at the end of life? Had I nothing more to offer? Sometimes I sank into such moroseness that the coffee would grow cold, and then, when finally roused from torpor, I would down it in one gulp, almost gagging, nauseated, but somehow feeling righteous in acceptance of this medicine, this just punishment for weakness.

The day after the interview with the principal, thinking to take advantage of what would surely only be a few days of enforced leisure, I went to the barber's for an overdue trim. The barber, who had cut my hair for twenty years or more, chose that day to tell me that my hair was thinning on top. He brought out a pair of mirrors, and there at the crown of my head my hair was visibly in retreat. No doubt I had been losing hair for some while, but at the time it seemed to mark a sudden loss of youth, of vigour. I was, I despaired, being swept into premature senility and impotence. If only I had known how far from true impotence I still was then. I did have the power of my youth, I could have acted, but thinking too much aged and enfeebled me.

After lunch at the coffeeshop, I would return home and await Rani, who most days would be back by early to mid-afternoon. Now instead of cherishing her independence, I was irked by it, for I found myself sliding into dependence. The day was marked off by her departure and her return. Although I still had savings, it was her income, her work, that supported us now.

The first day that I went to the market she chided me for buying a fish, an *ikan tenggiri,* that was not fresh. It was true. When she pointed it out, I could see that the fish was yellowing at the gills. But I could not stop the frustration pouring from me, and yelled, telling her to buy her own fish, that I was not her servant, not stopping even when she shrank back, alarmed by my vehemence.

To reach the market I had to pass by a patch of open ground. One day in that first week away from teaching duties, having forced myself to rise earlier, anxious to avoid settling into the lazy routine of the idle, I passed that patch of grass while it still glistened with dew. It was not the dew that drew my attention, but a host of yellow butterflies, whose fluttering seemed to present me with the ever-changing patterns of a kaleidoscope. I paused to admire the sight, uplifted by the miracle, commonplace though it might be, that metamorphoses caterpillar into butterfly. It seemed to hold the possibility that anything might change, that the world itself could be transformed, ugliness turned inside out into beauty. That day, however, the skies darkened after my midday meal and the wind begin to stir in anticipation of an afternoon storm. Passing by the butterflies on my way home, I was sure that their dancing flight was less lively than before, and wondered how they would survive the lashings of wind and rain.

Around this time too I went to see my parents. Walking towards our old house, I noticed how the neighbourhood had deteriorated in the last few years. Many members of the community had left this area around Short Street for Katong or elsewhere. Some of the old houses had been subdivided by their new owners, and now seemed overcrowded with tenants whose respectability was definitely open to question. I had told my parents of the suspension already, over the telephone, but they still seemed startled to see me in mid-morning, as if only now did they understand the significance of what I had said. Father, who had retired only at the end of the previous year, appeared the more uncomfortable to be seated, before noon on a working day, in his front room with his adult son. Mother, after her initial rush to the gate in a brief frenzy of maternal anguish, seemed less concerned. She disappeared into the kitchen, happy to be preparing coffee for both her men.

I looked at Father, resenting his full growth of hair. Where did my incipient baldness come from? I guessed from my maternal grandfather, whom I had met only as a baby, when my parents had returned on holiday to Ceylon, a year before Mercy was born. Mercy had told stories of him, of the time she spent with him during the War. She had spoken of his shiny bald pate, and how he wore a topi out of doors so as not to burn his precious scalp.

Father was looking back at me, a sad, worried expression on his face.

"What can I do to help? Is there someone I can go and see?"

There was pain in Father's voice. Puzzled by it at first, I gradually understood its cause. Father wanted to protect his son and was dismayed that he could not think of any way to do so. He had walked, that day after the Japanese captured Singapore, all those miles from Tiong Bahru to Lim Chu Kang, walking to assure himself that his wife, and perhaps more importantly his son, whom he had placed out of harm's way, were safe. He had taken upon himself the risk of staying to protect our property, in that initial phase of Occupation, for the sake of his son and heir. But now, when he had already retired, believing that I was securely placed in a good job, with a future full of promise, now he was called upon to gird his loins once again and save his son. Then he had protected me by a burst of physical effort. Strength of heart and force of will were the twin pillars of his life. But now the world had changed. Father did not know what to do. Indeed there was nothing he could do.

Seventeen

Krishna called from time to time, telling me that, since things had cooled down a little, he could arrange a meeting with the Ministry. All that was needed was for me to disavow the opinion expressed in the article, not publicly perhaps, but at least in writing. "The good thing, Abraham, is that you're nothing, the smallest of fishes." He accepted my refusal to back down, even saying that he respected me for it, but was skeptical when I insisted that I could successfully defend myself before the committee. At other times Krishna tried to break my malaise. "At least stop brooding. Come out once in a while." I preferred not to, though I gladly allowed Rani to go out with him: to the cinema, or just for a meal. She needs the break, I thought, away from me. I tried to shake off my mood, but found it easier to resolve to do so than actually to do it. Disappointment suffused me: whether in the world, in Krishna or in myself, I was not sure. Perhaps all three. One night Krishna even took her to an official function, some affair at one of the embassies. "You know me. No time to chase women. And she'll enjoy it."

Finally, a few weeks after my suspension had begun, I was notified of the date on which the committee would sit. Together with the notification came a formal statement of charges. To my surprise, there was no mention of the article. Instead, I was accused of insubordinate and insulting behaviour towards the principal, and of leaving school without permission during the middle of the day, when I still had classes to teach.

At first, I was almost giddy with relief. Some mistake had been made. It would be relatively easy to answer these charges. I had not been insubordinate or insulting towards the principal. I had behaved with great restraint and deference. As for leaving school, why, there were plenty of witnesses who knew that I had tried to teach my one remaining class that day. I had been prevented from doing so. I decided to sort things out straightaway and telephoned Chong, the teacher who had taken over that class. He was friendly, asking what I was up to and expressing the hope that I would be cleared by the committee and return to work soon. But when I explained the situation and said that I expected him to come forward and state what had really happened, the sparkle left the voice on the other end of the line.

"I really can't get involved. You tell them what happened." The voice was dull and flat, shorn of all emotion.

"But you're an independent witness. I need you. Just to tell the truth."

"I have to go now. Please, don't ask me to be a witness."

"I believe that I can ask the committee to order you to attend. You're a teacher. You're under their jurisdiction."

"Abraham, I have a wife. I have children. I have to, you know …"

"What?"

"Toe the line, lah. Come on, Abraham … you know what it's like."

"You mean you'll lie. How can you? You're a Christian. You pray to God on your knees every Sunday." In spite of myself, agitation shook my voice.

"Hey, don't get abusive. Are you trying to make me say things for you?"

"That's a goddamn lie ..." But it was too late. Chong had put down the phone. I put my head in my hands and swore softly. Rani was passing by, going to the kitchen to bring out the plates to set the table for dinner. I reached out to her, taking her hands in mine. She kissed me, lightly, on the forehead, and gently removed her hands. Her touch could not ease my bitterness against Chong. The man was a Christian, yet he would lie. This paradox led me to reflection that evening. The problem, I felt, was that while Christianity threatened hellfire to those who did not do right by their fellow men, it held out too easy an escape route. All one had to do was to repent, to pray for forgiveness, and it would be granted. So Chong could believe that, in spite of his cowardice, he might avoid unpleasant consequences both in this world and the next. This had to be a misconception of the doctrine of repentance. A man must be judged by his actions towards his fellow men, not by the extent to which he abases himself before the Lord. Christ must have been deliberately misunderstood by generations of clerics playing to a constituency of the rich and powerful, who had to believe that they could postpone truly embracing Christ until their deathbeds.

The difficulty lay in the fact that in the Bible, even in Christ's words alone, there was material for a dozen different theological positions. I began to believe that interpreting the Bible was in itself a barrier to understanding, and tried instead to read without the constant flow of analysis and commentary that normally accompanies any study of the Scriptures. This was harder to do than I expected, and I only achieved anything resembling success when the passage seemed so directly aimed at my situation, a man beset by his enemies, his faith tested, that exegesis became evidently unnecessary.

The next day two of my pupils called round after school. I had been lying on the sofa, eyes pressed shut in my despair, and had come blurry-eyed to the front door upon their knock. I was surprised to see them. One of them, an Indian Muslim boy by the name of Mustajab, was from the class I was alleged to have abandoned, and I was even more surprised when Mustajab told me that he had heard about the committee and the charges, and that he would testify to say that I had indeed attempted to teach that class and had been prevented only by the order of the principal. I shook Mustajab's hand warmly, and gave them ginger beer and fruitcake before they left.

The committee was convened for a Saturday morning. The venue was St George's, in the meeting room next to the principal's office. I was there early, dressed in a light blue shirt and patterned blue tie. Rani had helped me to choose them as the appropriate attire. She should have come with me, I asked her to, but she said she would be of no use and would simply make me tense by her own nervousness.

As I was about to leave she asked me again to seek Krishna's help, this time telling me to make any retraction that might be asked for. Anger swelled within me, perhaps for a reason I did not then divine. "Have you no faith in me? Must we run to Krishna for everything?" I left the house without kissing her goodbye.

So I was there on my own, confident that I could put to rest the misunderstanding. Trust young boys to do the right thing. The thought calmed my agitation. When the principal arrived I made a point of nodding politely to him, greeting 'Good morning' as the man scurried into his office. Although Mustajab was not there yet, he would turn up soon enough.

The committee arrived together at exactly nine o'clock. They must have rendezvoused elsewhere. There were three of them.

One was a member of the Board of Governors, a tall Chinese gentleman with a large waist and, it seemed, a chain-smoking habit. He was a doctor, Dr Yong. With him was a small Chinese woman who apparently worked at the Ministry, although she hastened to add, smiling at me, that she was not serving on the committee in her official capacity, but as a private individual. The third member was an Indian. He had a broad face, but a sharp nose and small shifty eyes. I guessed that he might be Sindhi, and was proved correct when he identified himself as Mr Gulwani. He said quickly, and somewhat aggressively, that he had sent three sons to the school and donated a lot of money, and did not want to see standards slip. I felt that I already had the woman on my side, and that she might be the one to win the others over.

Dr Yong began the session.

"You understand the charges brought against you."

"Yes."

"And you do not accept their truth?"

"No."

"The principal has told us that he does not believe that you are fit to remain as a teacher here, in view of the charges made against you. Have you anything to say?"

"They're just not true. I was never abusive to him. And I wanted to teach my class. He stopped me. He ordered someone else to take over."

The woman from the Ministry was smiling. She looked sympathetic. She asked in a gentle voice that I tell them what had happened. I did so, addressing my remarks towards her, realising as I did just how pretty she was and feeling a renewed surge of gratitude that there was at least one member of the committee with an open mind.

"That's all?"

"I did have a witness. One of the pupils in my class. He saw what happened."

"Where is he?"

"He should be here by now. May I go out and take a look?"

"Please."

I stepped out of the meeting room and walked to the staff room, looked inside and then walked towards the main entrance to the school building. Mustajab was nowhere to be seen. I returned to the meeting room.

"He's not around. I don't know what happened to him."

"Don't worry. Never mind."

The woman from the Ministry was still smiling. She had told me not to worry. They must have accepted my explanation. Then she spoke again, continuing in that soft, reasonable tone of voice. "I'm afraid we really can't believe you. I know that the Ministry would not have tried to interfere or put pressure on the principal. Your writing that article was ... well ... not really our business, so long as your work or your relations with the other teachers, or the administration, was not affected. But your making this allegation against the Ministry, now that's serious. You're trying to smear us. Suggest dishonourable motives. That's no way for a teacher to behave. We have to believe the principal after what you've said today. He called you in for a quiet, calm discussion about, well, the implications of the involvement of a teacher in politics, and you — and I think we've seen first-hand your tendency to overdramatise things — you overreacted. You shouted at the poor man. We can't have that. What kind of example is that for our children?"

Her eyes widened as she looked enquiringly at me. It was the sort of expression a woman might put on to rekindle her lover's desire, so that the next moment she could place a gentle but firmly restraining hand against his chest. I stared back at her. I could think of nothing to say.

"Now, the next thing. Abandoning your class. You say you wanted to teach them. But there were forty pupils there. None of them has come forward on your behalf."

"I didn't want to involve them. And one pupil volunteered."

"Yes, this mysterious missing pupil. Mr Isaac, we're quite prepared to give you the benefit of the doubt as to the pupils; children can be unreliable. But there was a teacher present. Why didn't you ask him to come forward?"

"I did. He refused to come."

"We could order him to come."

"I told him that. He said he would lie."

The woman's eyes widened again, distracting me once again with their inappropriate, and presumably unintended, coquettishness.

"That's another serious allegation, Mr Isaac. Now, this man, Mr Chong, has given us a statement, in which he says the principal asked him to take over the class after, I repeat, after you had left the school. He also says that you threatened him subsequently. That you were the one who wanted him to lie."

"Can I see the statement?"

"I've told you what it says. You don't need to see it. Well, do you have anything to say?"

"He's lying."

Air escaped from her mouth in a soft whistle and she turned to the other committee members, shaking her head.

Dr Yong had the last word. "Mr Isaac. Thank you for coming down. We will confer, and you will of course be told of our recommendation. Good day."

Eighteen

I catch sight of myself in the mirror just before I put in my dentures. I curl my lips around my gums and laugh. Before that first lesson with Richard, I was so nervous, so excited at the opportunity to teach Latin again, that I forgot my dentures. It was a miracle the boy did not scream in terror!

I first noticed the recession of my gums, the roots of my teeth gleaming white like fresh tombstones, soon after I was notified that the committee's decision had gone against me and that the grounds for my dismissal, which had been made effective from the date of my initial suspension, was serious misconduct. This meant that I received no notice or pay in lieu of notice. The committee had taken all of three weeks to reach their decision: were they pretending that they had given the matter careful deliberation or were they simply lazy? A week after that notification the Ministry informed me that my licence to teach had been revoked because of my dismissal by St George's. From then on I could only give private tuition, to groups of nine or less.

It was around that time that I first felt, with the tip of my tongue, the gap between the smooth enamel surfaces of my upper and lower canines and the soft flesh of my gums. Looking then at my teeth, running my tongue around them, then glancing at my thinning hair, I wondered if my dismissal would accelerate the deterioration of my body, so that I would fall apart within the year, like a wooden puppet whose string had been cut. What after all was I without my job? What claim on life could I have?

One evening, after we had finished dinner, Rani hesitantly suggested that it was time for me to start looking for pupils to tutor or perhaps for another job altogether. She mentioned the possibility of my finding employment as a clerk in a law office. Her sincerity was manifest, but I took offence. Later I realised that what had sparked my resentment was her seeming readiness to accept that I could no longer be a teacher. Her matter-of-fact proposal of practical alternatives seemed calculated to make the injustice that had been done to me appear commonplace, hardly worthy of protest. How could I meekly accept my fate and start looking elsewhere for a job? I had to rage, vent my grievance and my hurt … and that I did, shouting at Rani for the temerity of her suggestion, until she sat cowed and silent at the table, not daring another word.

Why did I not reach out to her? Why did I cloister my heart within the walls of my pain? As a youth, I had, once in a while, and never for very long, contemplated the possibility of becoming a monk. It was a great calling, perhaps the purest, the finest of all vocations, yet I had always, in the end, turned away from it. It was not the asceticism that repelled me, far from it. The truth was that, as I read Benedict's Rule, the concept of abnegation thrilled me. To deny the self, to dedicate one's being to a higher presence, what could be nobler? I sensed the danger in such feelings, as Benedict did, for mention of abnegation was always followed by a call for moderation. The man who flagellates his body may exalt his soul, yes, but may do so in false pride. Benedict's common sense convinced me that, in the modern world at least, one's life would yield the greater good if turned towards the practical rather than the spiritual. But, as if monastic reclusion still beckoned as an ideal, I had come to feel, in my isolation, that abstinence could be the only course of action. But abjuring her body, I had unwittingly spurned her soul.

Or was it only lack of vigour, the dissipation of vital energies by the tedium of empty days? Goaded by her apparent helpfulness, her guileless suggestions, that night I was stirred to potency. After we had both prepared for sleep in silence, she smarting under my temper, I still resentful of her advice, my loins burned for her. It was not just desire, but also dominion, the need to prove myself still master of her body. I turned to her in the darkness, pressing myself to her, hard against her belly. She pushed me away. I caught her arms as she did so and held them, reaching forward to kiss her.

"No," she said, turning her face away. "Let go. So long you've ignored me. Now you want me."

I turned onto my back, gazing upward at the ceiling.

"Darling, I've had so many problems. Forgive me for my temper."

To my surprise, she was crying.

"Rani, Rani, what is it? I'm sorry."

Silence, except for her sobs, and then, as they slowly died away, not even those. I turned towards her again, reaching out a hand to caress her face. This time she did not brush me away.

"It is I who should be sorry, Abraham."

Fear gripped my heart, as the meaning of her words took shape in my mind. Surely it could not be.

"You have seen another man?"

Her silence was my answer.

The name sprung to mind fully formed, as if it had been hidden only by the flimsiest veil, now sundered by lightning.

"Krishna. It can only be Krishna."

Again I knew from her silence that I was right. Time seemed to have stopped in my heart: I felt nothing, except that this must be a dream.

"When? Why? He forced himself upon you? The bastard."

"No, God, no." It was the first time that I had ever heard her use His name in this way.

"Talk to me, dammit, talk to me. How can you just say such a thing and then keep quiet? What am I supposed to do? Do you love him, is that it?" A void opened up inside me. What do you do when your wife, on whom you have built your life, confesses her love for another man? The Bible is simple, direct. Have her stoned for her infidelity. But what was that except a loser's response: destroy what you cannot have? What does the modern man do, what ought he to do? John Stuart Mill, Bertrand Russell, all the texts of my modernity — none held even the beginnings of an answer. Nor, for all my learning, did any of the Latin poets: reading Virgil, Ovid and all their number had not prepared me for this. All that came to mind was a passage from Erasmus, comparing the folly of believing a pumpkin to be a woman, a folly derided by the world as madness, with the folly of seeing the beauty of Penelope in your wife, an everyday folly thought evidence of love, the highest of earthly sentiments.

Silence. She would not answer. I reached for the lamp. At least see her face, know what she thought even if she would not talk. The burst of light shocked her, and she turned away from it, away from me. Roughly back towards me, hand gripping her upper arm tight, her skin whitening around my fingers.

"Talk to me. Do you want to go to him? Is that it?"

Fear in her face, voice. "No ... yes ... I don't know ..."

"You don't know. If you beg my forgiveness, that's one thing. Maybe I can take you back. Or you go, leave me. I can survive. But don't tell me you don't know. As if you're asking my advice. I can't advise you on this."

"I love you, but …"

"But what?"

"But there's something missing … something."

"And you couldn't tell me this? You used to say how much you loved me, how you couldn't live without me. Have you forgotten?"

"No."

"I think you've forgotten."

"I haven't. Sometimes … things change. You've changed. You sit and brood. When do you think about me?"

"So what are you saying?" She dared tell me I had changed. Virgil, warning of the fickleness, the inconstancy of all women, a warning that Mercury presses upon Aeneas, urging him to fly at once from Dido, Queen of Carthage, Aeneas' beloved. Aeneas has chosen, chosen to do his duty, by his men, his nation and his destiny. A painful choice, for him no less than for Dido. His choice has thrown her into despair. Mercury warns him that Dido's despair may at any moment swing to outrage and anger, to the command that his ships be burned and he and his men slaughtered. Another woman putting her narrow, selfish, sinful desires above the dictates of duty and honour.

The ancient gods and the Bible unite in their frank acknowledgement of the shortcomings, the essential weakness, of women. I was convinced, momentarily, of the truth of an ancient belief, namely that no woman can be trusted, and was certain that its truth had been wrongly obscured in this age of so-called reason. Even Jesus had not said that an adulteress should not be stoned. He had merely commanded that the first stone be thrown only by a person without sin or fault. Rani tied to a stake beneath a hot Middle-Eastern sun, and myself there too, taking up the first stone, for where was my fault? What had I done to deserve this betrayal? Yet, even as the vision took shape in my mind, I recoiled from it. A great sorrow took its place.

"Krishna wants me to leave you ... to go to him."

"And you ... do you want to go?"

She did not reply. "Rani, if there's something wrong, I can change ..." My voice cracked. "Stay with me. Tell me at least what you want to do."

"I love him, Abraham. I will go."

I released her, sinking back into the bed. That was not what I had wanted to hear when I had sought her answer.

"Rani, please ... think about it first."

"I have. I'm sorry."

"Tell me ... that time you asked me to seek his help, remember? As I left for the committee?"

She nodded.

"Had you already ... you know?"

Again she was silent. "So you asked your cuckolded husband to beg your lover for help? So that you could both laugh at me?"

"No," she cried, "You don't understand, you're not even trying to understand." But it was too late. The anger was boiling within me. Was it then that Rani got up from the bed? Or sometime later? What I do remember are her eyes, her eyes wild and rolling. She left the room, going to the bathroom. Some minutes later, the front door opened, then slammed shut. Her footsteps, running down the stairs, yes running, as if I were a demon she had to escape, echoed in the emptiness of the room. I made no attempt to stop her. To do so would be pointless.

How did she find it within herself to betray me? I had been a good husband to her, providing Christian leadership but in the most modern way: by example and inspiration. Rarely had I chided her or stood in the way of something she wished to do. Yet when I was down, when the world pressed upon me, she did such a thing to me.

For a moment I am flushed with righteousness and self-pity, but then I am awash only with sorrow, tears pressing against the backs of my eyes. Rani, come back to me.

Her face stares up at me, that impish smile, those glorious eyes. I slam the photograph face down on the desk, as hard as I can, savouring the pain that shoots through my fingertips.

Nineteen

Seeing Krishna on the other side of one of the narrow lanes off Serangoon Road was a shock. He had not yet spotted me and, oblivious to my presence, was crossing the street, a Govindasamy Pillai plastic bag in his left hand. Blood rushed to my head, my vision blurred, and I turned to avoid the man. Yet even as I did so I could not resist looking back, noting the grey hair and exposed temples, the slack skin around his once sharply mocking jaw. The man was in bad shape, worse shape than me. Little wonder perhaps, but still it thrilled.

I relished the moment a second too long, for Krishna looked up and caught my eye. Confusion clouded his features, and then they cleared into a smile, his body turning, his hand reaching out. I hesitated, torn between embrace and snub, hesitating until my uneasiness was apparent, so that Krishna too halted, his smile hinting at an old, quizzical amusement, watching and waiting for others to commit themselves first. That brought the bile to the back of my throat and my feet back to life. I did not look back again.

How many years ago was that? And why, whenever it replays in my mind, do I feel the grip of melancholy settling upon me? What regrets can I have? Krishna was the one who should have spoken, it was he who chose to hold back.

Time and age never solve things, never heal old wounds. Perhaps they only wear us down, until the pain, set against our general weariness, seems quite inconsequential.

There is another ache, that of conscience, the yearning to do what is right and good. That pain still throbs, but indistinctly, muffled by the tiredness seeping through my bones. How can a man, enervated by the years, keep his path true, his passage straight? Even the revolutionary fervour of those old men of China, aging patriarchs of Communism — even that has been dulled by a like process, until the energy of youth has become an enemy, a threat to order, an unseemly challenge to the certitudes of life: that the poor will always be with us and power in the hands of the few.

The strange thing is that in those first years in Katong, change seemed inevitable. Old imperialisms had been shattered by the struggle against fascism. How could they resist the fresh thoughts of a new age? Or modern man not shake off his feudal servitude, rise up to assume responsibility for his own life, reason inevitably become the chief shaper of the new world? Only later did I understand that the great ally of authority, the enemy of change, of progress, is distrust, distrust of those around us, the man standing at the street corner, the woman hanging out her washing next door. Who can be sure that reason will prevail amongst his neighbours, or be certain even of its dominion within himself? And if not, then it can only be prudent to prefer regulation to freedom, dictatorship to democracy.

Was it Katong that deceived me, in those heady days of my youth, sensual and romantic Katong, with the sea beating on the shore only a few hundred yards away? The mansions that had the best sea views and the largest gardens, hosting the most extravagant parties, ablaze with lights and the shimmer of cheongsams, how could they last? Or resist the demands of all those who thronged the wet market at Siglap or crowded the *kopi*-shops along Tanjong Katong Road?

Beehives and cat's-eye glasses. Slim women in tight cheongsams. How can I not regret having known so few women? If nothing changes, if all that endures is the old and weary, hunched and diminished, then not to have lived more fully, to have read the works of philosophers when I could have danced, written articles when I could have … could have what? I would not have known how to in any event. Few might have read my opinions, and none might now remember them, yet what else could I have done? Temperance, not desire, was in my nature. If I am to find meaning, it must lie in that, that careful planning of a life's work. That I may have fallen short is still no reason to lament a life undiverted by hedonistic pursuits. Perhaps the true value of a good life lies in its aim, not its trajectory.

And after all I have Victor, have brought Victor into the world. To have a son, a fine, upstanding boy, is that not legacy enough? It is vanity for a father to consider himself unfulfilled, vanity that is tantamount to blasphemy. But what has Victor inherited? What can I point to in myself that endures in him? Is there anything?

That's a silly question, neither fair nor helpful. Surely I have grown beyond this, this anxiety to justify each of the many turnings that my life has taken. When I was in my forties, with so much unachieved, misgivings were understandable, perhaps even natural. But am I not yet reconciled to the fact that much of my life has been charted by other pilots, that both map and wheel lay all too often beyond my grasp? And that this must inevitably have been so? Doubts about marriage, friendships, politics — surely those belong to middle age.

My face has aged, but is still the same face. More and more my features resemble Father's, although I have never achieved his girth nor the inexorable collapse of chin and cheekbone into wobbly flesh. I have kept trim, can even boast that I am slimmer than

Victor. There's a man for whom prosperity has speeded up the years. I have, in short, fared well, maintained a good bearing without even a hint of a stoop. That my breath comes in gasps whenever I climb stairs, well, what man of my age breathes easier?

Still I cannot dispel the feeling that I have lost my youth without ever really living it. Desire, passion, the very sap of youth — for me they were creatures of the mind and no more. Rose escaped, then Rani. ... I never allowed desire to seize me, to carry me away. How much happier to be Augustine, repenting a misspent youth, than to be Abraham, mourning unconsummated passions.

In those first days of loneliness, without Rani, yet too proud to return to my parents' household, my meals were taken in one or other of the many eating places off Serangoon Road. Male territory, where labourers, their wives and families in India, come daily for refection. I took a strange consolation in food, looking forward to *dosai* or the curries steaming in aluminium pots. The pleasure of that first mouthful after the day's listlessness: of itself it seemed enough to make life worth living. Yet those meals always ended in surfeit: I would order too much and could never curb my desire to prolong the food's pleasure for just one more mouthful.

Surfeit brought nausea. I quickly understood that it was a mere matter of discipline. My fall from grace had, I was sure, rendered me easier prey to baser, coarser instincts. The nausea was simply punishment for forsaking the asceticism on which I had prided myself. In time I learned once more to eat less, even amidst that abundance, even side by side with a labourer whose banana leaf was piled high with rice and *sambar*. Yet in doing so I lost the pleasure in food that had, for a while, blessed or cursed me, I know not which.

The truth then must be that pleasure and excess are corollaries. One cannot have one without the other. Moderation my touchstone, how could I ever have succeeded with women, for whom the senses must always count more than the intellect?

Watching the large rough hands of a labourer smacking up his meal with the palm of his hand, distaste was quickly followed by admiration. Both attitudes were less mine than inherited from Father. Father had extolled the virtues of a simple life, yet had taught us the power of the word, and bred, in me at least, a condescension towards, perhaps even disdain for, those who lived only by the sweat of their brow. The cringing greeting of the gardener, fingers to forelock in that universal gesture of subservience, seemed the natural foundation of our universe. Much as I rejected such hierarchies in my mind, still I remained infected by the prejudices of my parents. Only by an act of will did I daily resist the urge to take the *dosai* from the serving tray with my own hand, rather than let the server, dressed in a food-besplattered singlet and sarong, seize and carry it to my banana leaf. It was not reasons of hygiene that dictated this urge: intervening at this late stage in the course of the food's journey from stove to table could make no difference. No, the urge came straight from my parents, from their insistence that all food prepared outside the home must be unclean, impure or both.

We inherit only the worst from our parents: prejudices, fears, guilts and inhibitions. For the admiration I felt for the labourer came also from Father, and sprang from guilt that I could never be as strong. Father may have put on weight, his muscles slackening with the years, yet still there was something in that bulk which betokened strength. Had not the man always condemned me as a weakling, despised the job of teacher first of all, then the shameful way I had been unmanned by wife and best friend and finally my meek endurance of all subsequent humiliations?

As a child visiting the home of some family friends, I paled at the sight of a glass case filled with butterflies, displayed impaled against velvet backing. The case had been brought out by the man of the house to amuse or amaze his visitors' children, and he took ill-concealed offence at my horror. Father considered the incident a personal shame, the son's squeamishness reflecting on the father's courage. In later years, once, playing cricket, when I hesitated between taking a second run or settling for just one, ending up by being run out, again when I refused to take any steps to expose Krishna's liaison with Rani during the time that Krishna was still a man in the public eye, Father called me, in a quiet voice, as if it were the most common or garden insult, a butterfly.

What fruits then has my life borne in Victor? A distrust of women, a fear that at their hands lies only humiliation? A disdain for my own idealism, seeing my dreams of participating in some grand project, some all-encompassing endeavour, as the surest sign of weakness? Far better to look after one's own, to stand one's ground. Contempt perhaps for all my agonising over right and wrong, a preference instead for action, in fulfilment of desire. My love of Latin, what has that become in Victor's eyes? An imposition, an irrelevance? The boy has no time for the thinkers of the past, the present, he says, is just moving too quickly. In whom lies the folly?

Twenty

*V*ictor's car draws up by the side of the road nearest to my block. He reaches across the front passenger seat to open the door for his father.

"Sorry I'm late. Office kept me back."

"No problem, isn't that how you say it these days? Work must come first."

"I thought we could try this new Indian vegetarian place. Supposed to be *dosai* served in style."

"Sounds like we may have to pay a lot of money for the style."

Victor grins, but does not suggest another restaurant. His eyes are intent on the road. A spot of dried blood mars his white collar. He must have cut himself shaving this morning.

Why does he still keep up this weekly ritual, this solemn feeding of his father at moderate to expensive restaurants? Is it just a token of kinship, given without respect or affection, or does he really hold some love in his heart for me? That would be something, would it not? Something to show Rose when she comes, proof that I have not lived in vain.

When Victor was born, Rani was already living in a flat near the Botanical Gardens. The rent was no doubt subsidised by Krishna, but he would not, it appeared, take the step of living with her, presumably for reasons relating to his political reputation. Was it honour that held him back from love? Residual stirrings of a code he had all but lost? Or did he not truly love her? Did she abandon her honour to love him, only to find her love unrequited?

When she told me, hesitantly, over the telephone, that she was pregnant, I reacted angrily. What business was it of mine? They could sort out the problems of an illegitimate child on their own. Why hadn't they thought of that earlier, taken the necessary precautions as I had always done? I threw back at her the words that she had uttered soon after our marriage: "No baby for a few years. Let's learn to live with one another first."

Then she told me, firmly, bitterness creeping into her voice. The baby was mine, she was convinced. How could she be sure, I asked, hearing a plaintive note enter my voice. But with her sharp reply that I should not ask such a foolish question came a dancing, radiant thought. I have a son, my mind raced, correcting itself, no, a child, perhaps a daughter. Why shouldn't she be sure? For the first time in many, many months, happiness surged through me, I wanted to shout, to scream, *"Look at me, I'm not a failure, I have a son, I mean a child, there, growing, in his mother's womb."* But I did not shout. Instead I spoke calmly.

"I will take you back, for our child."

"Is that what you wanted? A child to force me home?"

"Rani, no. Don't say such things. The child, perhaps he is a miracle, a sign. I will forgive you everything. Come home."

"I'm thinking of having an abortion."

She put the phone down. I shouted into the mouthpiece, then redialled. Her number was engaged, she must have taken the phone off the hook. What should I do? Go to her flat and plead with her? Or swallow my pride and speak to Krishna, my best friend and enemy, something I had so far refused to do? Krishna would see reason, and, if she would listen to anyone, she would listen to him.

152

I called his number. Krishna picked up the phone and recognised my voice immediately.

"Abraham, this is a surprise. You know that I've wanted to speak to you. I've been in pain too. It hasn't been easy."

"I'm not calling about your pain. That is not my concern. I want you to stop this abortion nonsense."

"Abraham, there's not even a Bill yet. It's just the Prime Minister's thoughts so far."

It took me a moment to follow the misunderstanding.

"I'm talking about Rani."

"Is she pregnant?"

"She hasn't told you?"

"I expect she was about to. I've been rather busy lately."

"Look. I don't care how busy you've been. It's one thing stealing my wife, another thing killing my child."

"Hold on there, Abraham. Wait a minute. First of all, it has to be Rani's choice. I can't stop her from doing something she insists on doing. Secondly, how do you know it's serious? She probably hasn't realised that it's not easy to get an abortion. If she tries an illegal abortion that's dangerous. For her, I mean. Once she understands that …"

"I don't need a lecture, Krishna, from you of all people. Just speak to her. And when the time comes I'm going to fight for the boy's custody."

Whether she had ever meant to seek an abortion, I would never know, but she did not have one. I did not learn of Victor's birth until the day after, when her father called with the news. I rushed to the hospital to catch a glimpse of my tiny, wrinkled son, and insisted on naming him. "Let's avoid the Bible. And hope that this name will help him triumph over the circumstances of his birth."

153

My parents, and Rani's, attended the baptism, nodding politely at one another but avoiding conversation. Rani's father, I knew, had taken my side, urging her to return to me, until silenced by her mother, who was adamant that she must know some dark and terrible secret of which they remained unaware. Krishna did not attend, although in different circumstances he would have been an immediate choice for godparent.

Soon after Victor's birth, for the first time in my life, I consulted a lawyer. Gopal, in fact, former classmate and smart-aleck. Whenever I think of him I think first of his mimicry of the Australian soldiers newly arrived to defend Singapore. How apt that he should don the robes of the advocate and spend his life playing to the gallery for other men's causes. He was then in partnership with two other lawyers, a partnership that, at least from the evidence of his well-appointed office, was prospering. He hunted when he could, driving north to Pahang and Trengganu to stalk wild boar. The stuffed head of a boar was mounted on a wooden shield behind his desk. He was sympathetic, but discouraging.

"It hurts me to see this. I remember your wedding as if it were yesterday. But I suppose it's for the best. Right." Gopal put his glasses on. "Now, first of all, the law has just changed. Divorce is easier. One of the benefits of self-government." He chuckled, stifling the chuckle when he saw that I had not responded.

"Secondly, custody really doesn't depend on who was at fault. It depends on the interests and welfare of the child. When a young child is involved, it's a fairly clear presumption that the child will be better off with the mother. Later on, the court will want to preserve the status quo. The only way things might change is if Rani goes through a rough patch, has mental problems or something."

"Right. So I lose."

"That's the grim reality. But you should protect your position. Come to an agreement with her. For example, get her to agree that she can support herself. Limit your support to the boy. And get her to agree to giving you as much access to him— Victor, right? — as much access as possible. You have something over her after all — she's the one at fault, not you."

I thanked him for the advice. It had been sound, to the point and kindly meant. Still, I regretted having consulted him. I would have preferred someone whom I did not know. Talking to a friend about my failed marriage was humiliating and shameful. Perhaps it was not so much admitting to an unhappy marriage that brought on my shame as the fact that it had been her, not me, who had been unfaithful.

I spoke to Rani, and a few days later we met at Gopal's office to sign the deed that had been prepared. I would be entitled to see Victor every Sunday afternoon, but at other times only by mutual agreement. I would pay to Gopal every month a fixed proportion of my income, to be invested by him on Victor's behalf. Advances from the fund could be made for the boy's maintenance before he reached maturity, whereupon he would be entitled to the whole. How much were the legal fees, I asked, and was surprised at how touched I felt when Gopal, waving his hand dismissively, told me that it was quite enough if I covered his disbursements, such as stamp fees and the like.

I soon found some pupils to tutor, most of whom were the younger brothers and sisters of former students. My income was satisfactory, I could not complain on that score, but I suffered grievously from the diminution in status. No longer was I the teacher, respected by children and parents alike as the oracle of learning, the judge of a child's worth and ability. Teachers were the human face of an educational system that sorted out the stream of uniformed boys and girls into doctors, lawyers, technicians and labourers. All parents wanted their child's teacher to be on their side, their guide to university and the professions. How much power a teacher wielded!

Now I was merely a tutor, paid to improve my charges' grades. If I failed to do so, the children would regard me as a failure. The parents would think me a fraud. One father, displeased with his son's results in the English 'O' Level, shouted at me, demanding his money back, for some reason only raising his voice when I tried, calmly, politely, to explain that the boy, not the brightest of sparks to begin with, was thoroughly lazy.

On Sunday afternoons I would go over to Rani's flat. There, under her watchful eyes, I would hold our baby. One of her unmarried cousins had come to stay and help with Victor. Neither would talk to me. Rani kept her answers to my questions monosyllabic, while her cousin would giggle at any remark, no matter how sober, and make no response to my substantive enquiry, whatever its subject. At first, Victor slept through all my visits, except for brief interludes of crying quickly silenced by Rani's nipple. But, as the months went by and Victor became less wrinkled and more lively, I began to discern the child's character: cheerful, intelligent, robust, with a taste for adventure. This last inclination was apparent from his equanimity, even his delight, when being twirled or held upside down. Victor, I would think to myself, as Rani bustled by, smoothing down antimacassars and tablecloths as if to accuse me of disrupting her life by my visits, Victor, you shall be stronger, cleverer than me, you will succeed where I have failed. Only later would I begin to believe that it was less any quality of robust adventurousness that kept Victor from crying than simple obstinacy. And with that belief would come the realisation that he would not be a son to inherit his father's mantle or pursue his father's causes.

Twenty-One

I would read about Krishna in *The Straits Times* from time to time. The man was only a backbencher, so reports of his activities were brief, albeit adulatory. But there were rumours of a break-up in the Party: the more radical members were dissatisfied with the pace of change. There was a sense that the Party's bold programme of import-substitution was not really working: the country continued as it always had, making money from the passage of goods and people through its port. Whose side would Krishna take? A breakaway faction could hardly expect to obtain power immediately, so anyone who went with them would risk the full-scale attack that must surely follow. Detention without trial could not be ruled out in any struggle, although some people believed the age of such barbarities was past, that detention without trial was a product of the transitional years after World War Two, when Britain was waking to the reality that she could no longer afford a global presence but did not want to deliver her former colonies into the waiting arms of World Communism. Such measures of control had no place in a democratic and almost fully independent nation, these people said, how could they ever be used by a party committed to Socialism and Democracy?

But I was certain that Krishna's assessment would be no less cynical than my own. How then could he risk breaking with the Party? Yet at the back of my mind doubts lingered. The man had always been willing to gamble, and after all must have reached the summit of his climb within the Party: if he stayed with them he would never be more than a backbencher. But if he chose rebellion who knew what heights he might achieve?

The split came and Krishna went with the dissenters. The size of the breakaway faction took everyone, including me, by surprise. In spite of myself, I felt caught up, for a while, in the excitement of this renewed competition for power, and once again, as so often in the past, I envied the man for his involvement, there right in the midst of the action on which Singapore's future depended. I had been too much of a dreamer, always drifting towards the periphery, worrying about inconsequential issues of principle. A man must act, seize his opportunity. Too soon the moment passes, and the rest of his life descends into wistful speculation of what might have been. I was convinced that Krishna must be a pivotal figure now, wooed by both sides, but working only towards his own advantage. The bugger had certainly relished a contest, certainly triumphed as far as I had ever been concerned.

Father urged me to find some way to punish Rani and Krishna: "The man has a public name to uphold. You can destroy him, tell *The Straits Times* of his adultery. Why did you not name the man in the divorce? Stand up. Fight back. You are a fool to give your consent to the divorce. Don't flutter away like some butterfly."

I did consider what Father said, but such a step would harm Rani as well as Krishna. It was only Krishna on whom I wanted revenge, or at least, with Rani, the moments of hatred passed quickly, to be replaced by longing and despair. Mother's counsel interested me more, even though I doubted the truth of the information on which it was based. She told me that she had heard that Krishna was trying to distance himself from Rani, that he saw her now less and less often. Mother did not know whether this distancing was prompted by a concern for his political reputation, or simply because he had grown tired of the girl. Perhaps he had even found some other married woman to pursue. She suggested that, if I really wished to take Rani back, if my heart was truly filled with Christian forgiveness, I should make another effort at reconciliation.

It was not that I did not want it, want it more than anything. Just that I could not bring myself to face further humiliation by acting on this suggestion. Instead, I tried to forget her, to find solace, at those times when I was not giving tuition, in reading. I reread the Bible, from beginning to end, finding much of it troublingly obscure. At times, however, I was uplifted, momentarily, by its promises. I have not failed so much that the path of salvation is closed to me, I would tell myself, yet doubts persisted. Faith is so difficult to hold on to, even at the best of times, and in those troubled days and troubling nights it seemed always to be slipping away. The Kingdom of God seemed so unreal that, at times, in the cool light of the early morning, sitting at my desk sleepless and alone, I could only conclude that it was imaginary, imagined, invented by men who had failed to achieve their mission in the real world, and who had to fall back on bogus claims of an afterlife where all their hopes and dreams would be fulfilled and their earthly foes condemned. These were men who could not find meaning for their existence within their own lives, so they conjured up a power without, outside the world, which power, in their fever and their despair, they believed could supply that missing meaning.

Retreating into myself, I took less interest in the world of politics. What did it matter that once full independence from Britain was assured debate almost immediately began over merger? I scarcely bothered with the accounts of negotiations between the governments of Singapore, Malaya, the United Kingdom, Sabah and Sarawak. Nor did I follow with more than cursory attention the divisions of opinion on the proposed merger, and its terms, between the Party and its breakaway faction. Politics was not for such as I.

One morning, glancing at the copies of *The Straits Times* laid out for sale on a street vendor's plywood table, I was shocked to read headlines about a massive security swoop. More than a hundred people had been detained. I picked up the paper to read the story, attracting the concern of the vendor, who demanded immediate payment. I paid and took *The Straits Times* to a nearby coffeeshop. Krishna there among them. My old friend. Emptiness opening up within me. An awful sickening wrench to my insides and then, suddenly, pleasure — his turn to suffer. But the pleasure faded, rapidly succeeded by guilt. Rani, I thought, and hurried home to call her, to see if she needed help. But she was hostile, bitterly accusing me of delighting in Krishna's plight. I denied the accusation, repeatedly expressing my concern for them both and my readiness, should Rani ever wish it, to take her back. Finally, when I thought she was ignoring all that I had to say, my frustration roughening into irritation, she thanked me and told me, in the politest tones, as if we were in truth strangers and I some gentleman who had held a door open for her or walked her across a busy street, that I was a good man to have telephoned her. It was pathetic, I told myself afterwards, how happy her compliment made me.

The next day a knock came at my door. I opened it to find two men, dressed rather shabbily in plain clothes, standing outside.

"Abraham Isaac?"

"Yes. What is it?"

"Internal Security. We'll step inside?" His words bore the inflection of a question but I was evidently not intended to have any option of refusal.

"Am I under arrest?"

The man who had not yet spoken, taller and thinner than the other (whose tightly stretched shirt revealed oval patches of tanned but corpulent flesh between the buttons) broke into loud abrasive laughter.

"Should you be? If you say so it can be arranged." He laughed again.

The other man, who had not joined his partner in laughter, addressed me in a soft, gentle voice that was perhaps intended to underscore the forces that he could unleash if he so chose. "You are, I am sure, guilty of many things. But our concern is not with you. You are a friend of P. Krishnasamy? You don't have to answer; we know. You were friends. You were colleagues at St George's. He was best man at your wedding. He entered politics. You lost your teaching licence. Then you lost your wife to him. All true so far?"

I nodded, mouth dry.

"Do you want your teaching licence back?"

I nodded again.

"Of course you do. I read your file this morning. You're a good writer, but misguided. I'm sure you were a good teacher. No, don't be modest. Now, please remember that if you cooperate this will show that you have regained the social responsibility that a teacher must have. Do you understand?"

I managed to mouth the word yes.

"So when I ask you to sign a little statement, it shouldn't be a problem, am I right?"

"Can I see the statement?"

"Of course. Read it." He handed over a sheaf of paper, a type-written statement, consisting of a top copy backed by two carbon copies. The statement was very brief, and simply expressed my recollection that while we had been colleagues at St George's Krishna had frequently discussed politics both in the staff room and in the classroom, and that on reflection I now realised that Krishna had been seeking to make converts to the cause of Communist subversion.

"But I don't believe that he's a Communist."

"But he used to talk politics often."

"Yes."

"And you know now that he's a Communist. Otherwise we would not have detained him. All you have to do is put two and two together."

I stared blankly at the man, vaguely noting the smallness of his eyes, a marked contrast to his puffy cheeks. To the left of his lips, now pursed in anticipation of an answer, was a mole, from which a pair of long, straggly hairs sprouted.

"I suppose not." My voice was weary, mind resigned to this last failure. I could not find the courage to speak, to say that everyone talked politics, at least back then, when fear of governmental reprisal had not yet begun to seep like some rancid discharge into people's minds.

"Then sign." He motioned for me to take from his hand a cheap ballpoint pen. "All three copies." I stared at the ballpoint pen, held by the man as if it were a dagger.

"No." Where did that voice come from? I thrust the man's hand away. "No, never. I will not be Judas."

"Come, come, Mr Isaac. Don't be dramatic. Rama ... I mean Krishnasamy ... he's no Christ. Look upon him as a sacrifice, a ram that must die — figuratively speaking, of course — for the good of the nation. We must show Malaya, and the British, that we can keep law and order, keep Communism in check. Krishnasamy is proof of our ability to do so." He was silent for a moment, studying my face. Then he began again. "In any case, it's better for him if you sign the statement. Then he'll realise that things are hopeless, that it's best to confess. The sooner he confesses, the sooner he will be free."

Until that moment I had wavered. Now I knew that I must not sign the statement. What, after all, could they do? I had already lost my livelihood. They were not likely to waste their time putting a man like me into detention.

"No, I will not sign."

To my surprise, the men accepted my refusal. No threats, no argument. They walked out of the door, the taller man saying that he would say "See you soon" except he was sure I never wanted to see them again. He laughed, harsh, guttural laughter, and knocked me on the shoulder before turning away. "Hope you're that lucky."

Krishna never confessed. Over the years I even grew to admire the man's steadfastness. It was easier to do so when he was safely behind bars, far from me. It was unexpected, really, such resoluteness, for I had begun to believe that the man was nothing more than an opportunist. But perhaps there was no inconsistency: perhaps he refused to confess, not from courage, but from a stubborn refusal to admit defeat, to acknowledge that he had backed the wrong horse. Or dare I think he addressed his obstinacy to me, in expiation, or towards the restitution of his honour?

Eventually, in the late 1970s, when his health was failing (he had developed some intestinal problem), he was released. By then, Rani, who had pined for him as if to spite me to the very last, had died, four years short of her fiftieth birthday. She had been worn out, not by Victor, who was always a quiet, well-behaved child, but, I believe, by two things: the constant detail of daily life that she had to face alone and the absence of hope that things might improve. She had been diagnosed a diabetic when Victor was three years old, and somehow always lacked the will and energy to fight the problems that diabetes brought in its wake. It was her kidneys that failed in the end. Yet in all those years, something, pride, contempt, I know not what, stopped her from returning to me.

After her death, Victor came to live with me. We seemed to get on with one another all right, although I had to learn to endure the occasional sullen silence, and the boy's obdurate refusal to accept that he might have got some fact about the world wrong. He stored the knowledge that he acquired like an arsenal of ancient weaponry, swords, maces and battle-axes, that he brought out mostly only to polish or display, but occasionally to wound or maim. As a teenager he would unleash a withering scorn on any classmate, even a friend, who showed himself ignorant upon any matter whatsoever. Perhaps it is this combination of tenacity and scholastic swordsmanship that has made him such a good lawyer. There is nothing visionary about him, despite his scholarship. He uses his skills to advance his career, inch by inch, head down to his work, accepting the world as he finds it.

The cutting of the engine jolts me from my meditations. I look across at my son as he opens the door, illuminating the interior of the car. Who can say that I did such a bad job? Is the boy not dependable, a good citizen? As for his pragmatism, that must have come from Rani, together with a spirit that on occasion shrinks into meanness. I can hardly be blamed for those failings. A wife would do much to counteract them, for the protection of one's wife and children brings out the best in a man, leads him away from selfishness. But why is the boy still showing no sign of interest in marriage? He has never, at least not to my knowledge, even had a girlfriend. "You work too hard," I say as I get out of the car. "I cannot be happy until you have found a wife."

Twenty-Two

The restaurant is much as I feared. The chutneys are bland, the *dosai* less than crisp and piping hot, and the quantity of *sambar*, itself rather tasty, meagre in the extreme. Few of the clientele are Indian. Why would Victor want to dine here? Has Serangoon Road become too redolent of *paan* and toddy, the bad habits of a backward past, too crowded with guest workers scrambling for a taste of their homeland? Or is it that here he can speak English and not be forced into a language with which he is increasingly unfamiliar? I always strove to ensure my son's fluency in Tamil as well as English. I even attempted to teach him Latin but quickly realised that Latin could not be forced upon such a stubbornly reluctant tongue. The boy rebelled, not just against Latin, but also against Tamil, applying real effort only when he knew that a good grade was essential for a university place. Thankfully he did not identify English with my strictures, or else simply recognised the overriding importance of the language, for had he not acquired mastery of it he would not be a lawyer today, commanding the respect and the fees of many of the most influential men of business.

That is enough; who am I to judge? Let him discard languages if he must. Perhaps the world, in any event, is tending ever nearer to the day when English, and only English, will be understood by all. Who am I to extol the benefits of learning for its own sake? Where has such vanity led me?

Over dessert, a *gulab jamun* that I have been unable to refuse in the face of Victor's insistence and a *kulfi* for him, I speak of Rose's impending visit.

"You must meet her, boy."

"I will. She sounds like such a fine lady."

"Not just that Victor. I didn't tell you before, but she helped me to pay your tuition fees at the U."

"I didn't know." Victor's face has darkened. "I am not happy to be indebted to a stranger."

"What do you mean?"

"How much did she give you? I will pay her back, with interest."

My son's vehemence is bewildering. What ideas possess young people these days!

"You will do no such thing. She would be so insulted."

"Why should she be?"

"Her reward is your becoming such a good lawyer. She'll be proud of you. Don't offer her money." In my distress my voice cracks. False pride that the young can no longer accept help from their elders.

"I defer to your age, old man. But I'm none too happy."

Victor insists on coffee for us both. I am again unable to refuse, although my mind has begun to wander with the tiredness that always assails me by this time of night. The taste of the *sambar* is still on my tongue and I drift back to the early days of marriage, when I would come home to the welcoming smell of *sambar* bubbling on the stove, a tub of batter ready by the side to make my favourite *rava dosai*.

Rani. I struggle to catch glimpses of her in Victor's face. He has grown too plump of late, but even that cannot hide the same slant of cheek and the suggestion of a pout that would be more pronounced had Victor not worn braces for some of his teenage years. That was an expense that I endured gladly then, for at times those young boy's lips, stretched across his thrusting teeth, reminded me too sharply of her. Yet now I rue the severance of one of the few links to her memory that were left to me.

"Your mother would have loved to see you married." The words are out before they have even formed in my mind. Beyond recall, they cause me instant regret. I must stop nagging the boy, I who built a marriage so little to be proud of! I expect vehemence to equal or surpass that of a few moments ago, but there is no outburst, just a wan smile, and the slow turning outwards of his palms, a gesture of such resignation that I am silenced.

Victor drives me home, fast yet unhurried through empty streets. We sit quietly without talking, Victor intent on the road ahead. I look out of the window at the passing shopfronts. They are interrupted only by service stations or road junctions until they give way to the housing blocks of my estate. At least here there are more trees, although these are dwarfed by the concrete buildings. Before long we arrive at my block. I unbuckle my seat belt, my nascent goodbye stilled in my throat by Victor's sudden breaking of the silence.

"You want to know, you really want to know?" His voice is harsh and rough, and I shrink back. "I'm not going to marry. You understand?"

I say nothing.

"I'll never marry. You're a modern man. You must understand." My son's voice has changed from defiance to pleading, yet my whole body recoils. The car is too small for both of us. The air presses down upon me.

"You're no son of mine, not mine."

I am out of the car and striding, breathless, towards the lifts. I am almost there when Victor catches up.

"How can you do this to me? Just walk away. What do you mean?"

"You really want to know?" The mocking words spring from my lips without a moment's thought. "You're not my son. I should have known. You are Krishna's boy. Go tell him what you are." I spit the words out with more distaste than I intended, for, as I speak, an image, a disgusting, nauseating image, grips my mind.

"What are you saying? Who's Krishna?"

"Why do you think I kicked the whore out of my house?" Froth is forming on my lips. "You are the unclean fruit of an unholy union."

The lift arrives, and I turn to enter it. As the doors close, my last glimpse is of Victor, his face drained of colour, his body motionless, cadaverous.

Twenty-Three

The night is restless. For some reason I am drawn back to my earliest memories, to days that seem bright and luminous in my remembrance. Days when Mother dominated the home, and Father was an unfamiliar, almost resented, yes resented, intrusion in the evenings. Mercy had not been born then, or had she? There I was clinging to Mother's sari, crying out for her undivided attention as she busied herself with cooking or housework. Life then consisted only in the contentment of a full stomach and the warmth of Mother's adoration. Days long past, yet I cannot stop my heart from aching for Amma, for her arms that would reach down and lift me to her breasts.

Drifting into troubled sleep in the early hours of the morning, I wake unrefreshed, my neck stiff from having fallen asleep with the pillow bunched askew beneath my shoulders. In the afternoon I catch a bus to Lily's house to meet Rose. I cannot invite her to my home, as I did on her last visit, for that room does not count as home, still less as one presentable to her. I imagine her house in England to be something truly grand, with its stone fireplace and iron firedogs, and wooden beams running across the ceiling. She told me in one of her letters a few years ago that they had moved to a converted eighteenth-century farmhouse, near Henley 'where they hold the regatta: bunting, tents and awnings, strawberries and champagne, and all the boats on the river.' With such girlish enthusiasm does she play the English wife of leisure!

Lily, as ever, remains aloof, leaving it to Rose to rush to the door at my ring, and, after the briefest enquiries about my health (I am much the same as ever) and requirements by way of refreshments (I have none), disappears. After a few pleasantries, expressions at how well the other is looking, we sit awkwardly facing one another, on opposite armchairs across a low coffee table.

Rose breaks the silence first. "Well, it's been a long time. Tell me how you are?"

Annoyed by the rich English timbre of her voice, I can manage no more than a slight shrug of my shoulders in reply. I take the initiative, anxious to deflect attention away from my own life. "And how's the English wife of leisure?" Too late I catch the undertow of bitterness in my question.

Rose looks at me, wide-eyed, surprised no doubt at my tone. Perhaps she is thinking that she has never understood me, and never will. As she speaks, the flabby flesh below her chin wobbling in a manner that reminds me all too clearly of her mother, I wonder how I could ever have been besotted with her. "Yes, fine. It is a leisurely life I suppose, with the boys working now, and Charles on the Bench. But it's not all strawberries and garden parties, you know. I've been very active with Oxfam, you know the charity. I don't suppose it's allowed to operate here, although why anyone should be afraid of middle-aged women from the Home Counties, I can't imagine. How can you put up with it?"

It is her turn to aim a dart at the balloon of my life. I do not want to waste the time we have together in this uneasy sparring. But how can I break this pattern that has settled upon our encounter?

"I was so pleased to hear of Charles' elevation."

Rose narrows her eyes in suspicion before thanking me, politely, as if we were strangers. She says that some had thought it a most overdue appointment, for he has really become pre-eminent in his field.

Silence overtakes us. We avoid each other's gaze, until at last Rose makes what she must suppose to be the final enquiry expected of her. "And Victor? I must meet him. He seems to be doing very well, from everything I'm told."

And though I have intended discretion, an intention strengthened by the posturing of our conversation thus far, I find myself saying "Then you have not been told everything."

"Whatever do you mean, Abraham?" Beneath the plummy depths of her acquired accent there has suddenly risen an old sympathy that I recognise. It speaks from my childhood, from those hours after choir, waiting for the adults to finish their gossip and retrieve us from games of catch or hide-and-seek with the other children. Or, especially as we grew older, from where we had found a quiet spot together to talk and put the world to rights. Suddenly the words burst forth in a torrent. I am barely articulate, yet she seems to understand, for she moves to the arm of my chair. Even in my agitation I savour her proximity, the warm smell, and slowly I, so long without woman, am calmed by it.

"Whoever is Victor's biological father, you have been his father all these years. You did him a great wrong."

"But ..."

"Who are you to think that your seed could not produce such as he?"

I do not speak.

"It is not for us to judge, Abraham."

I am scarcely listening. My mind cannot spare my heart the memory. If all these nights when memories weigh me down, nights whose frequency increases with the passing years, if they are to be more than just a torment, are to hold out the promise of expiation, I must face it squarely. My heart recoils, yet I force the memory to unfold from the depths of my mind where it has lain knotted for so long. A man must not flinch. He must either justify or repent. He cannot turn to his books, not even to the Book, for his answers, but must think for himself, think clearly, and with courage.

That night, while Rani still lay by my side, before she left me forever, I rolled onto her, pinning her down and pulling up her nightgown. "You bitch." Did I really use such a word, such a hateful ugly word?

It was the first time that I had taken her with the lights on, but I was sure that the pain and fear that dimmed her eyes had not been there on previous occasions. I pushed, thrusting deep, taking my time, until she moistened around me. "Does he do it better, bitch? Tell me, bitch." Yes, I used such words.

Release brought with it tears, as I rolled onto my back. I know now, if I did not know it then, obsessed with my pain, that in that moment I lost her forever.

I gaze through my tears, yes tears once again, up at Rose's face, still an angel's, hovering before me. Later perhaps I will regret this weakness in front of her, but now I am only grateful.

"Why ever did you leave me, Rose?"

"Abraham!" She begins my name in indignation, but ends in an old, familiar girlish giggle.

From Lily's I go straight to Victor's flat. This is not something that can be put right over the telephone. He is not here, which is hardly surprising, since it is still before seven. Some years ago I was given a key ("In case," he said) and thankfully I attached it to my own bunch. For the first time I put that extra weight to use, and, after opening a window and switching on a single standing reading lamp, I settle down in an armchair to wait.

Through the window comes the smell of onion and garlic from a neighbouring apartment, frying for the evening meal. How I will start, or what words I can find to express what I must say I know not. That I have done wrong is clear, yet how else did he expect me to react? "That's nice, son. Goodnight then"? Absurd, and intolerable. Thoughts of Victor, of sickening, vile lusts, still plague me. The fruit of my wicked union cursed, and I with him! Far from triumphing over the circumstances of his conception, Victor has been moulded by them. If a woman will lead a man to such wickedness, then far better to be with men.

For a moment distracted by the sound of a mother calling her young children to the dinner table, my mind returns to Victor. But is he truly my son? The doubt remains. How can I be sure? What about blood tests? Surely the doctors can tell me. Rani's face drifts towards me, and then disappears. My mind wanders in the half-light. Suddenly there in front of me is Krishna, his lips curled in that old mocking smile. Old friend, you've come back for me … Krishna, you supercilious old bastard, I should have signed. I would have had my old job. And Rani. Rani.

With a start I realise that I have been asleep for some time. No more smells of cooking or sounds of dinner. Everything seems quiet, and darker than a moment ago. The time? I peer at my wrist watch, an Omega Constellation that Rani bought for me soon after we were married. It's past midnight. Where can the boy be, on this a weekday night? I stand up, slowly, feeling the strain in my joints. Whom to call? Not the office at this time of night, and I have no idea whom else except the police, it was them after all who had found … I turn inside out in an explosion of panic. No, it cannot be. Not be. He would not be so foolish, a man who was so success-ful, so careful.

Still I find myself anxiously pacing the room, long legs carrying me too fast from one end to the other. And if it were, it would be once again upon my head! But that was David's fault, not mine, not mine. But this, whose else could it be? Oh God, oh God, oh God, faster and faster, oh God, oh God, in the rhythm of my stride. He is my son. Whether or not he is my son, he is my son. Let it not be him. Take me instead. Faster and faster, until I am losing my balance, about to topple, my head crashing towards the sharp edges of the coffee table. I place myself upon the altar, turn my neck towards the knife. Me, Lord. And Mercy, that ignored, forgotten phone call, my indifference, my washing of my hands, far worse than ever Krishna had. Mercy, the name burns with Victor's, breath comes shorter and shorter, sweat on my brow. That night when David and I drove, in a feverish haze, in vain search of Mercy. And how, after that, my heart burned with hatred of David, even as it ached with sorrow for Mercy. How is it that we are able to juggle such extremes of feeling with apparent equanimity? Why did my sorrow not cancel out the anger and lead me to forgiveness? I who talked of love and honour, and understood neither. Now it is as if the windows of my mind have been flung open by the rapid, wild striding of my body, so that the rough winds of my past fly unhin-dered within, scattering cobwebs and turning up the pages of memories. Mercy's laughter as that foolish pompous family at-tempted an aggrieved and dignified retreat — what was the name of that young man, Mercy's first suitor? Rose, motioning me to silence when I should have spoken — why ever did I not? What false meekness possessed me? Rani, smiling and saying, "How slow you are! Perhaps I watched you too much, like water that one hopes to boil on the stove." If only I had been slower, more steadfast, perhaps then … Infant Victor, his bright and inquisitive gaze fastened upon me. My son, and then at once the despairing question: what can I do, what difference can I make, except stagger from one end of the room to the other, impotent in my ignorance?

Calm yourself, Abraham. There must be something to be done. I stop suddenly, in the middle of the room, arms swinging crazily for a moment. Perhaps there's an address book by the phone, and I can look for names of friends. Start calling them. I walk to the phone, a little unsteadily, feeling giddy, for the pacing up and down has sent the blood rushing to my head. Yes, there is an address book. I pick it up and start thumbing through its pages, struggling to focus on and decipher the scribbled names, realising even as I do so the futility of my effort. I have no idea with which of the names to begin, which might be friends and which business associates. What will I say to the person who picks up the telephone if I begin calling numbers randomly? It's absurd, utterly and hopelessly absurd, and I drop the address book in despair.

In its fall it knocks over something else and I look down to see what it is. A framed photograph, knocked face down on the side table. I reach down to set it upright once again. And am arrested by the stern and forbidding gaze of a young man, the sort who is supremely confident of himself, a man such as Richard will become. Certain that his life will make a difference, mark a turning point. Yet inside, behind the flutter of brave words, will he be strong, or like me? If I could only begin again: not be frightened or ashamed of love, crippled by ancient notions of honour. Compassion, not righteousness, is the good man's backbone.

With a start I recognise the woman seated to one side of the young man, whose hand rests on the back of her chair. She is Rani, a faraway look in her eyes, a proud tilt to her chin. It's Victor's copy of the photograph that I misplaced.

176

The hand that without warning roughly seizes the frame sets my heart leaping. A heart attack, but then the palpitation passes, and I turn to face the apparition, mouth opening in my joy and calling "Vikki-boy". I freeze as I take in the frown, face darkened with anger, brow furrowed.

"What do you think you're doing here?"

"My boy ..." I cannot continue.

"Get out of here."

"Victor ..." Soft, pleading.

"Get out."

"I came to apologise." At last my numbed mind has found some words of utterance. They now pour forth in a torrent, as if I hope to convince by the speed of my diction. "I'm sorry. I should never have spoken as I did. It was wrong. Quite wrong. I'm truly sorry. Please accept my apologies. I'm sorry."

"Fine," says Victor brusquely, loudly. "I'm so glad. Now go."

With each passing moment the distance widens. Soon no words, no matter how fast their delivery, can hope to leap that gulf. I stare at that broadening canyon, seeing Victor lost like Rose, Mercy, Rani before him, myself all alone, entombed in my little room, and, like a man jumping from ship to shore, having broken free of the sweaty, grasping arms of the press-gang, I throw myself at my son.

"Forgive me. I have so much to tell you, to explain. You must understand. You are all I have and I love you dearly."

Victor's hesitation, battles fought upon his face. Father's voice in my ear, harsh, imperious, "Don't cry", disobedience visible in my eyes. And then, as if the age of miracles were not yet past, we are in one another's arms.

Standing here, arms around my son, breathing in the warmth pressed against me, I look around the room, lit only by the solitary reading lamp, and am at peace. I have done my best, and if I have

177

lived too much like a butterfly, soaring upon the puffs of my youthful fancies, too easily beaten back by the world's winds, well here in my arms is a beetle, clinging stubbornly to every inch of ground he gains. He may never change the world, hardly wants to, but still, head down, he will hold his ground. My grip tightens momentarily, and then we release one another, looking away in our embarrassment. What more could be asked of me? And what more could I ask of my son?

About the author ...

Philip Jeyaretnam first started writing while doing National Service — after discovering that one way of beating tedium is to describe whatever surrounds you in the minutest detail.

He graduated from Cambridge University in 1986 with First-Class Honours in Law, and readily admits that he spent most of his Bar Finals year writing his first book, *First Loves,* a collection of short stories describing the adventures of a young dreamer growing up in practical Singapore. His second book, *Raffles Place Ragtime,* is a short comic novel and satire of life in the big city.

Since 1988, Philip Jeyaretnam has been labouring on this book, interrupting his legal practice to indulge in some globetrotting, on a Fulbright Fellowship to the University of Iowa International Writers' Program and Harvard Law School, as a guest to the Melbourne Writers' Festival, to the Cambridge Seminar courtesy of the British Council and to Germany courtesy of Interlit 3. In between stops, he has found time to write a handful of short stories, including *Inheritance,* which appeared in *New Voices in South East Asia* and was translated into German and published as *Das Erbteil* in *Neue Metropolen,* and *Making Coffee* which appeared in *South East Asia Writes Back!* He is married and lives with four cats.